I0539254

Dan DeVeronica

Visit my website at www.SickBoy-thenovel.com

Printed in the United States of America

First Printing: December 2013

The Lost Press

ISBN-13: 978-0615900216

ISBN-10 : 0615900216

10 9 8 7 6 5 4 3 2 1

AKNOWLEDGEMENTS

There are a lot of people that this novel wouldn't have been possible without. First, my parents Jeff and Ruth DeVeronica. Thanks for giving me every opportunity to pursue my dreams. My wife Holly, you gave me the drive and determination to keep going when I thought all was lost. The original 1247 crew, you all know who you are. Melissa Greco Lopes, I quite literally could not have done this without you. Your help and guidance throughout this process has been invaluable. I'm forever in your debt. All of the writers over at The Cult of Chuck Palahniuk's Writer's Workshop. I miss The Cult greatly and wish you all the best. Thanks to Jake Alkofer, Vince Louis, Michael J. Fox, Bob Urwin, and Nathan Williams. The best friends a guy could ask for. And everyone along the way, friends, family, coworkers, you have all inspired me to write and driven me in so many ways, thank you. And Al of course, wherever you are buddy, I hope all is well.

For Holly, my wife, my life, my love.

Sick Boy

ONE

I can't sleep; the air in this bedroom is stale. Leaving fingerprints in the frost on the glass I slide open the single pane window next to my bed. The furnace clunks on with a hum and compression forces in a blast of icy air. I kick the beige feather comforter off me, bunching it up at the foot of the bed. The red glow on my digital alarm clock reads 4:45a.m., 15 minutes before I have to wake up for work. Normally I would be sleeping right now, but every time my eyelids shut the nightmare returns. An overpowering stink of iodine. Chilled surgical aluminum pressing against my backside. A powerful examination light giving me a slight migraine and forcing my eyes open. I'm sitting on a metal table; my hospital gown barely tied shut. The heavy brown door swings open and in walks my neurologist Dr. Shephard. He lowers the clipboard. His lips move, putting together sounds but nothing else. Puzzle pieces of words I know but can't recall. Then I wake up. And I remember. My hand fires like a bullet towards the snooze button, aiming to kill the blaring sound that rips away my last chance at blissful sleep. I grab a pack of cigarettes off the nightstand; it is time to get up.

I navigate through the living room in darkness making my way to the sliding glass door. Barefoot on the snowy patio, I light a cigarette and sit in a brushed off but still wet Adirondack chair. Inhaling the first drag of the day, I hold it in as long as possible. I should call my mom, but I don't. I breathe, think about my dream. There is a pounding thunder in my head, from lack of sleep, I hope. Slouched in the chair with my feet up on the patio table, warm drops of blood drip from my nose and pool on my bare chest. I should call in sick to work, but I won't. This dream is my psyche's way of coping. Yesterday, when Dr. Shephard opened his mouth he shut down my life. His words resonate like the echo of a gunshot inside my soon-to-be cavernous skull. *Your tumor is cancerous.* My tumor he called it, like a filthy stray that follows me home, he assumes it belongs to me. Planting my feet in the inch-deep snow I flick my cigarette butt over the railing. Within seconds my toes start to ache from the bitter cold. Pain is one small experience among millions I have taken for granted. Embracing it I go inside to get ready for work. It is time to start the first day of the end of my life.

I flip the small business card over. Written in cursive is a note from Dr. Shephard, barely legible, it reads: *First Methodist, 740 Maple Ave. They can help you.* They can help me is what he told me right after he said he couldn't. But I have to try something. The knots in my stomach tell me this is the right place. It looks more like a one-story office complex than a church. Just past the foyer there are some people wearing rainbow-colored shirts that say *You've got a friend in Jesus.* They guide me to the carpeted stairwell that leads to the basement. I can't help notice the array of Jesus portraits hanging on the walls. There is a Caucasian Jesus. An African-American Jesus. An obscure East Indian Jesus. There is even a Samoan Jesus. They all stare, condemnation in their eyes, as I make my way to purgatory; down carpeted cement steps into a basement that buzzes not with life but with fluorescent lighting. There are two ugly brown card tables on either side of the stairs. The dingy rusted kind my grandmother would setup in another room for the kids on Thanksgiving. One has pamphlets about different cancers and the other has a stained white coffeemaker, some Styrofoam cups, and a bulk can of generic coffee grounds. A large circle of metal folding chairs are in the center of the room. Five decrepit people are hanging out by the table but stop talking as I make a cup of coffee. A few people sit in the folding chairs waiting for the meeting to start. A young woman sits alone on the far side of the circle. A skeleton in a pale Saran Wrap, she is wearing a loose fitting outfit and an ugly multicolored do-rag that hides her bald head. She looks like she is in the final stages. Her eyes are laser focused on the cracks in the cement floor. I decide it's best to sit next to her. She has already travelled the road that I am heading down.

"Hi, how are you?" I say, my hand extended in greeting.

She doesn't break from her staring contest with the floor. After an uncomfortable silence, it is clear she doesn't want to talk and I remain quiet until the meeting starts. A few minutes later a fat middle-aged woman in a Red Cross t-shirt comes downstairs and asks everyone to take a seat. Her face is cratered with past scars of prepubescent acne picking. A born loser, who only exudes any control in her life here, over the cripples and invalids that society has forgotten. She stands in the center of the circle turning as she talks, attempting to face everyone at once.

"Good evening, everybody. Although most of you

know me I do see a few new faces in the room tonight. It is always wonderful to see newcomers."

Wonderful? If you're coming here it means you are dying. It is obvious that some gears are missing in that fat head of hers. And that voice. Peppy and kind in a way that smothers you. She continues to speak, slow as if none of us understand English.

"My name is Sally. Welcome to our home." She continues, signing "I love you" with her pudgy hands. "Now, without putting anyone on the spot, if one at a time our new comers could stand and introduce yourselves that would be wonderful."

Her eyes scan the circle. "Hmm, let's start with you." Her sausage link sized index finger points at me.

This is it, moment of truth. The first time I will utter the word cancer outside of the doctor's office is going be to these strangers. People that have no idea who I am or where I'm from. People who have no reason to care, other than the fact that they want me to care. But they are people who can keep my secret. I stand with shaking, sweaty hands and glance at the faces around the circle. A burning fire in my stomach rising to the back of my throat.

"Hi, everyone. My name's Dave. I have stage two brain cancer. My doctor said the tumor is inoperable." There are a few mumbled hellos and uncomfortable waves from the people around the circle. That's it, it's over. I collapse into my chair, exhausted to get such few words out.

"Well, Dave, on behalf of our family, welcome," Sally says, signing the word with a smile wider than her chunky face allows before moving on to her next victim.

After introductions Sally hands out a worksheet and tells us that these are questions to ask during tonight's sharing and caring activity. Whatever that is. The paper has 20 bland getting-to-know-you questions. Stuff you would ask when you are speed dating. She tells us all to find a partner and even in this safe container, behind the cement walls of the church basement, a social hierarchy is still present. There are cliques that form, people look to one another when Sally mentions partners and they break off, pulling the metal chairs to their own secluded parts of the room. All the while the corpse girl next to me sits alone; no one looks at her but me. Like at work when the employees avoid the next one to be fired, people gravitate away from death. I wonder to myself, how many nights has she sat here alone? Who is your partner when nobody's left? Then I notice Sally waddling over, her crosshairs set on this pathetic creature. Maybe she will want the three of us to be a group. I can see a shudder shoot up the frail girl's spine when she sees Sally coming for her. I have to do something. Standing up, coffee in hand, I move to intercept. Halfway between them, I trip over my feet and fall forward, sending piss warm coffee sailing through the air onto Sally. Her nose scrunches up and her double chin merges with her neck as my drink rains down, staining most of her red shirt a dirty brown. She freezes, her hands in the air as if she is being mugged.

"I'm sorry."

Through clenched teeth she tells me it is okay, she has a change of clothes in her car. She goes upstairs, babbling orders to the groups before leaving. I take my seat next to the dead girl and for the first time, I can see a smile on her withering face.

"Why did you do that?" She asks, still looking at her lap.

"I had to save you somehow," I smile. "How many times have you been forced to partner with her?"

"Too many, hero," She giggles, extending her hand. "I'm Katrina."

I shake her hand. It has a limp sadness to it, boney and fragile.

"I'm Dave. It's nice to meet you."

Her hand rises to her forehead to brush phantom bangs out of her eyes. She looks at her lap again when she remembers they are not there.

"Well, how about we get to these, partner?" I say waving the paper in front of her. I scan the list of generic questions until I find a good one. "Where do you work?"

"I don't work anymore, I'm on disability. But I used to work in a boutique downtown selling jewelry and stuff. It was the best. How about you?"

"I'm a middle management schmuck. It's alright, not what I pictured myself doing with my life. Especially now, being sick and all. Okay, your turn."

She doesn't hesitate. "What's one thing you want to do with your life?"

"Tough question, you go first, I need to think about this one."

"Fine, cheater," She smiles. "Enjoy every sunrise. I love sun rises."

"Good answer. I'll have to take a pass on this and move to the next." Scanning the list with my index finger, I notice she is staring at me. She leans forward, placing her hands on mine.

"Please Dave, don't worry. Share yourself with me."

Her smile, her blue eyes, and her sweet voice get the best of me. Something about her makes my heart shake.

"I'd like to see more of the world. Go on a road trip, go to Europe or Australia. But, I guess that dream is out the window now."

"Don't say that, you can't lose hope, hope is all I have left. It's all that keeps me alive."

"Uncomfortable," I say. "Next question." I scan the list again but pause when I see she is staring at me with a big smile. "What?" I say, startling her out of her trance, but not breaking her smile.

8

"You. You're different from the usual people we get here. You just say whatever pops into your head. I like that, you're fun."

"Why thank you Katrina. And to think, you didn't want to shake my hand."

"Oh yeah that. Well, I'm not good at making friends." She looks at the concrete floor, bouncing her right leg up and down.

"Well, let's get back to these questions then. Tell me one of your flaws," I ask with an innocent smile.

She fidgets with her blouse for a bit before answering. "I told you, I don't form bonds well, at all. I don't trust easily." She starts scratching at her arms and then begins bouncing her leg again. "Okay, your turn. One flaw."

"That's easy. I hate people."

"Do you mean people in general or certain people?"

"I think people in general. Well, the masses I guess. Take this room for example. You sit alone week after week, forced to partner with Mother Superior, over there. And, here you are one of the sweetest people I have ever met. It doesn't make sense."

She blushes and looks at the ground for a second, then her eyes roll up in her head and she falls forward out of her chair. I lean in to catch her frail body and lower it to the ground.

"Hey, can I get some help over here?" My cry causes

everybody in the room to stop and look at us.

Katrina's body flops and convulses, smacking against the concrete floor. The other members circle us joining hands. Frustrated, I hold her head in my hands and whisper that everything is going to be all right. Sally leads the maniacs around us in prayer, not lifting a finger to help this poor girl. My stomach is in my throat, it's all I can do not to puke from fear. I keep telling her that it will be all right. A few more eternal minutes pass and she stops convulsing. Her body goes limp and her eyes open, a smile widening across her face.

"Are you okay?" I say, still whispering. She blinks, her smile morphing into a grimace.

"Get away from me." She scrambles to her feet, backing out of the circle while everyone applauds.

Katrina takes a seat in a metal folding chair while her left hand recovers a colorful handkerchief from her purse in time to catch a nosebleed. With her head tilted back to stop the bleeding, she fishes out a bottle of pills. Ignoring the rest of the group I sit next to her and try to help.

"Here I can open those for you."

"I said get away from me. Now."

Still in shock from what happened, I plop into a different seat, but spend the rest of the meeting glancing at Katrina. One minute she likes me, the next minute she tells me to get away. I have to know why she is like this.

The meeting ends with us giving one another hugs. It's

10

weird. After making rounds to say goodbye to these strangers I catch Katrina as she is walking up the stairs.

"Hey, can I walk you to your car?" I ask, hurrying after her.

"I don't have a car."

"Oh, do you need a ride somewhere?"

"No." Unflinching, she continues up towards the door. I hurry past, opening the door for her.

"I'm not sure how to do this, so, do you want to get coffee with me?"

She halts, blocking the doorway and clenching her fist. "You know, support groups are not the best places to pick up women." She coughs hard into a balled up tissue produced from her sleeve.

"No it's not like that," I interject.

"Dave, stop. I'm not trying to be morbid, but you'll learn. Don't get attached to anybody you meet here. We have a somewhat short life expectancy."

"But Katrina, I..." Stuttering and stammering and interrupted I stop speaking.

"I had an interesting time getting to know you tonight, Dave. And thank you for your help with my little episode. Maybe I'll see you here next week, but if not, I understand."

Having said her peace, with a fake smile she turns and walks out the door into the snowy night. Seconds later a slew of people come charging up the stairs and out the door I am still holding, each one thanking me as they pass. Of course the last one to leave is Sally and she latches on to me. This shit always happens when I am in a hurry. She smiles without saying anything, tears filling her eyes as she locks me in a powerful bear hug. The steel door slips out of my grasp slamming shut. I'm trapped.

"Oh David! It was wonderful to see what you did for Katrina tonight."

"Yeah, thanks. Look, I have to get going."

"She has such a need for someone's love and support." Sally says, ignoring me. "But I must tell you," She leans in close trying to emphasize the importance of what she is going to say. "Because of liabilities, we have a hands-off approach when a member has a seizure. I know you're new, so we can let it go, but next time please just join us in prayer."

"Fine." I reply, my smile forced. "So you just stand by and watch?"

"We put them in God's hands."

In desperate need of a drink I squirm out of her grasp using early morning work as a scapegoat. Walking out of the meeting into the cold winter air both chills and revitalizes me. Maybe I took a major step in my life tonight. Or maybe I'm hanging out with people like me to feel normal. I don't know. I unlock my car and start to get in when I hear someone yelling my name. My heart flutters and I get out looking for Katrina. Then my heart sinks inside my chest. It is not her running towards my car; it is Sally, waddling fast and waving a piece of paper high above her head. I get in and crank the key. My piece of junk car stalls. In a second she is tap-tap-tapping on my driver's side window. I roll it down an inch.

"Take this, it's our phone directory. This way if you can't make a meeting or if you need someone to talk to, we are right at your fingertips."

I pluck the paper from her beefy pig hoof and toss it onto the passenger's seat. My car fires up, its engine shattering our uncomfortable silence. I say thank you without looking at her, put the car in drive and leave her standing alone in the night.

I arrive home a little after 10:00p.m. The roads were powdery with drifting snow and it took me longer than it should have. When I pull up outside my place I can see my friend, Nick, waiting in the cold with a 12-pack. His short dark hair is speckled white with snowflakes. He's sitting on the front step smoking a cigarette. Side stepping him with a hello I open the door and we go inside together, plopping onto my black leather couch.

"How long have you been waiting?" I ask, taking a beer.

"It doesn't matter, I love winter. What have you been up to?" He pops the cap off his bottle with a lighter and takes a long sip.

"Nothing, running errands. You ready?"

"Sure as shit, been waiting all day for this," He says, picking up his controller.

We drink, smoke, talk, and play video games for the rest of the night. It is our Monday night ritual. Tonight, I spend an hour telling him about a special girl. But not when or where we met no matter how hard he drills me. We drink until we pass out.

The mismatched morning scent of stale beer and cigarettes awakens me from my depraved slumber. My eyes burn as I rotate them inside their dried out sockets. The table is littered with empty beer bottles. We finished off Nick's 12-pack and everything in my refrigerator. I passed out on the couch, I think around five in the morning. Nick's gone, which is normal for him, I only hope he was sober when he left. I turn the television off and go into the kitchen for breakfast. My head is screaming, my legs ache, my mouth tastes like an ashtray and my cigarettes are gone. Beer hangovers are the worst. I wash down some aspirin with a cup of coffee and look at the time; it's noon. Two scrambled eggs, a burnt piece of toast, and three cups of black coffee later I'm in the bathroom brushing the foul taste out of my mouth. In the mirror I study crusty blood rings around my nostrils. They form lines along my top lip and run into my mouth drying on the front of my teeth. I thought my eggs had a coppery taste. Maybe this achiness isn't from a hangover. I shrug it off, shower, change, and leave for the day.

I head east for a half-hour, driving on slushy, winding roads as I navigate through the small town where I grew up. A few more turns and I pull into the driveway. There's always a sense of calming peace when I return here. A massive taupe farmhouse stands against the backdrop of thick snowy woods. To the right a frozen pond borders a steep, sloped hill where dense pine trees were bulldozed, providing a clear view from the backyard. To the left is a giant garage where my grandfather spends most of his time tinkering with trucks.

My parents had me too young to properly care for me, not that they didn't try. It was my grandparents who were always there, to pick up the slack right where they were needed most. A lot of kids these days barely get two parents, I was lucky enough to have four.

As I walk through the front door into the kitchen the comforting smell of fresh coffee and cigarettes enters my nose. It's the smell of every childhood morning. A smell I took for granted. Lucky for me it is so ingrained in the walls that after everybody quit smoking it lingered, surviving two paint jobs and new linoleum.

Across the kitchen, sitting at the table in her usual spot, is my grandma. Her pink bathrobe and old blue slippers perfectly accent the cluttered environment surrounding her. On the counter, a miniature television set airs the local news. A police scanner sits on top of a stack of old bills and news papers on the microwave stand, blaring out local calls. The screeching Morse Code dots, the monotone of the local meteorologist, the constant hum of the oxygen tank, none of these noises bother me. These are the sounds of home. An oxygen mask is sitting on the table next to a plate of toast. Her stringy gray hair dangles in front of her face as she hovers over a half-finished crossword puzzle. I walk over, pick up the mask and take a deep breath. The purity of the air is intoxicating. After a slight dizzy spell I sit in the chair across from her.

"Shouldn't you be wearing this?" I toss the mask onto the table.

"Only when I need it," she smiles, takes off her thin metal reading glasses. She brushes her long bangs behind her ears. "You're going to need it too if you don't quit smoking, David."

"I already did," I lie, smiling back.

I hear her call me a liar as I get up and go into the living room to fetch the Scrabble board from under the couch. The box is more of a sandwich, torn at the corners and faded from years of use. The dictionary is around 20 years old and I'm pretty sure some of the letter tiles are missing. This is what we do. This is the same game we have played year after year. I am only close to a handful of people. I've had more acquaintances than real friends; mainly work buddies and people I run into from high school. The two people I am closest with are my grandmother and Nick. My parents are a close third.

I spend the next few hours talking and catching up with my grandmother. We play Scrabble and she beats the hell out of me twice. She fills my ears with gossip about a family that I could not care less about. I do the dishes for her when we are done playing and make a small grocery list of what she likes and needs. All the while she continues with the gossip.

"You know, your aunt walked in on him and he had his dick in the sink," she says bursting into a combination of wheezing, coughing, and laughing.

"Serves him right for using aftershave there," I say through my own laughter.

As the laughing dies down there is a brief moment of comfortable silence and I decide it's time to tell her the truth.

"I met a girl, Grandma." The words echo off the kitchen walls as they leave my mouth.

"Oh thank God, you're finally over that bitch."

"She wasn't a bitch, she was—"

"She never treated you right. I never said anything ill about her while you were together and I always welcomed her, but I knew she was going to hurt you."

"Yeah, can we not talk about her? I am trying to tell you some good news." Sternly I redirect our conversation. I love the woman but senility easily pushes her off on tangents.

"Sorry. Go on, tell me about her." She puts on her oxygen mask, maybe to get some air or maybe to prevent herself from interrupting me.

"Well, I met her the other night and we talked and got to know each other. And I like her, a lot. But when I went to ask her out she seemed unsure of me." I stop there, deciding against revealing the whole truth.

She takes off her mask, readying her reply. "You be persistent. I didn't want anything to do with your grandfather the first time we met. Keep at it, you're charming and if you get her out once, she's yours."

"Alright Gram, thanks for the advice," I chuckle. "I should be going though."

"Oh no, that was such a tease. You can't go, tell me more," she begs.

"Well, who knows, maybe the next time I come over she'll be with me." I stand up and kiss her forehead, tell her I love her, and head out the door.

This is the way it has to be with my grandma. She hates it when I leave and would keep me there talking forever if she could. My grandfather spends most of his time in the garage and our family rarely visits them. It's better to say goodbye fast and leave than to draw it out. But then again, isn't that always the best way to say goodbye, fast?

I wade through the drudgery of the rest of the week only to end up running late on the one day that means something to me. The heavy aluminum church door swings open but there is nobody home. The Jesus freaks have left for the night. I hurry down the stairs and barrel through the basement door, startling a massive group of people. The setup is different tonight. There are 10 rows of five folding chairs each spaced perfectly. A man standing behind a cracked and peeling wooden podium stops talking and looks at me. All of the people turn around in their seats to face me. I don't recognize one person from last week. I open my mouth to ask where I am and the man in front preemptively interrupts me.

"Come in my brother! There is always room for another in our flock," he says, opening his arms toward me.

Everybody starts to clap and he motions for me to take a seat. I don't want to be rude so I sit in the back row. I scan the crowd but find nobody from last week. As the host leads the group in prayer, I begin to realize what is going on. The room is full of middle-aged men. I continue to study them; red blotchy faces, disfigured bulbous noses, sunken eyes, plastic coffee mugs in each hand. I know what this is. A shaky hand squeezes my shoulder in support from my left. This is a fucking Alcoholics Anonymous meeting.

Fifteen uncomfortable minutes later I frantically rifle through a week's worth of fast food wrappers on the floor of the passenger side of my car. Underneath the trash is the Mountain Dew stained phone directory Sally gave me. I look down the list for Sally's phone number to give her a call and find out what happened to our meeting this week. I begin to dial Sally's number then I freeze, looking at the list. No part of me wants to spend the next hour stuck in my cold car talking to Sally. I scan the list again, stopping at Katrina's phone number. My stomach flips and flops as I dial. If she doesn't want to talk she won't answer. The phone rings while I wonder why she got mad at me last week when I was trying to help. My gut has developed a mind of its own, twisting and wrenching, reflecting my anxiety. Maybe I should hang up and go home. Maybe she is busy, at chemotherapy, or having a nap. It may be best to leave a message. But before I can she answers.

"Hello?"

"Um, hey Katrina it's Dave from group."

"Dave? How did you get this number?"

"Sally gave me the phone directory last week." There is a long sigh and then silence. "Okay, well I was calling because I went to group tonight and found an AA meeting. Is something going on? What happened to group? Was it canceled?"

"Oh no, not at all. We had group on Monday. We alternate every Monday and Friday to accommodate other support groups. Sorry nobody told you, it's so weird that Sally forgot. She's not usually like that."

As strange as it may sound, this feels like fate. A maternal control freak remembering to give me the call list but forgetting to tell me the group schedule. Katrina's home, and answered the phone. With the fear of rejection still burning in my heart from the end of last week's meeting I launch into my next question.

"Hey, would you be able to meet me somewhere tonight? I could pick you up if you need a ride."

"Dave, I'm hanging up now, I'll see you next Friday."

"No, Katrina, wait. Something happened to me today and I need to talk to someone." I hope that didn't sound as desperate as it felt. She lets out another exhausted sigh before replying.

"There is a Starbucks at the corner of Monroe St. and Tenth, meet me there in an hour."

Why couldn't she have named one of the hundred bars near the corner of Monroe and Tenth? I have been sitting at a tiny round table by the window for about 25 minutes. Sitting here with sweaty palms and twitchy nervous hands, nursing a coffee that tastes like ass. I don't understand how places that specialize in coffee can brew such a variety without mastering plain coffee. Regular Starbucks coffee tastes like ass. The place was packed when I arrived but the crowd has thinned. The only people left are the two girls sitting behind me in big plush red chairs, a woman cranking away at the next great American novel, and a creepy guy in horn rimmed glasses pretending to read Chaucer.

I hate coffee shops. There is something to be said about the people that hang around them. Pretentious, unrealistic, and snobbish. Pretend intellectuals. Fake. I prefer the dank atmosphere of a small bar over these ultramodern social hubs any day. The patron saints of the barfly lifestyle are more practical. They are real people dealing with real problems, not sitting around fretting about the environment and global warming. That said, I guess a coffee shop is a neutral place to meet someone of the opposite sex. A bar or a restaurant could say, *hey, let's fuck,* but a coffee shop says, *hey, let's talk.* And so I sit, among people I detest, waiting for a girl who must think I am a creep.

My eyes are locked on the giant glass window to the right of the storefront as if I know which direction she will come from. Then, on cue, Katrina passes in front of the window. She is wearing a pink skull cap over her do-rag, a black pea coat, and blue pajama bottoms that disappear into black boots with faux animal fur around the top. She shoots me an awkward smile and waves as she orders her coffee. A few seconds later she sits across from me, her coat still on. We sit for what seems like forever without saying anything but hello. Staring at her in silence, I work up the courage to say something, anything. If only to keep from feeling like a creep.

"Why are we nervous?" I ask.

"What makes you think I am nervous?"

"Well, you poured 16 creamers in your coffee. Nobody, I hope, uses that much creamer."

"Oh," she laughs. "Well, why are you nervous?"

"Four reasons."

"Oh? Indulge me." She folds her gloved hands on the table next to her grande Americana.

"Okay, well, you showed up that's reason one. Two, this is only the second time we've met. And three, the way you acted at the end of the meeting last week scared me. Good enough?"

"I guess so, what's the fourth reason?" she asks.

"I'll keep that to myself," I smile, taking a sip of my ass coffee.

"Fine, then why did you call me?"

"I had a frightening experience at work and I need someone to talk to."

"And you needed me? Instead of calling one of your friends or your parents or maybe a sibling, you needed to call a stranger?"

"Look, I thought this is what support groups are for." I put a strong emphasis on the word support, sounding it out like she is hard-of-hearing. "But if you're uncomfortable this wasn't my aim. I need someone who understands what I am going through, not my parents and sure as hell not Sally." I stand up and put on my leather jacket. "If you have a problem with this I'll go and wait for group on Friday."

I pick up my coffee and start to leave. My inner voice is screaming at her, praying she will have a change of heart. Hoping to God she will give me an inch to foster this connection. Pushing open the cool glass door of the coffee shop I hear my name. I stop, turning to face her, brandishing my best poker face. The one that shows her how emotionless I am and that she means nothing to me. I could walk out right now and be fine. She hesitates, leaving us both facing each other like two gunslingers in the Old West.

"Excuse me," A female voice teaming with impatience snaps from the left. It's the snobby novelist from the corner. "I would like to leave." I move out of her way without breaking my gaze on Katrina. The woman mumbles something about us being rude under her breath.

"Come back and sit down," Katrina says.

I wasn't expecting that, but it's good to know that I still have a mean bluff. Slowly I return to the seat across from her.

"Thank you," I say, without a smile.

"I'm sorry. What was it you wanted to tell me about?"

"I had my first real episode since I was diagnosed."

She leans in closer placing her hands on the bottom of her chin and her elbows on the small café table. "What happened?" She asks, her dainty brow furrowed under her skull cap.

"Well, I was sitting in our weekly meeting. Every manager in the building was there. Our store manager and district manager, basically all of my bosses and all of their bosses. I was asked to prepare a presentation on in-store theft. I set up my PowerPoint display and stood in front of everyone. I knew exactly what to say beginning to end; only the words wouldn't come out. I thought I was talking, it felt like talking, but words weren't coming out. After about two minutes of spouting gibberish I walked out of the meeting and went home." I put my head in my hands. Reliving the embarrassment is tough.

"Oh, you poor guy,"

She reaches across the table and puts her cold bony hand on mine. My stomach flutters at her gentle touch. I never even saw her take her gloves off. "I know what you went through. At my last job the same thing happened to me shortly after my diagnosis. I was with a customer, it felt horrible, but I couldn't leave, I had to wait it out. I thought I was having a stroke."

"At the boutique?" I ask.

"Yeah... you remembered."

"Wow. That must have been awful, waiting it out. I ran home like a little bitch. And I don't plan on going back until next week at the earliest. I'm sorry you had to go through that."

"Thanks," she says, taking a sip from her coffee.

"Why did you get pissed at me when I tried to help you at group?" I blurt out, denying my own internal censor.

She chokes, spitting out a small amount of coffee. Remaining quiet, she picks up a napkin and dabs her chin. Afterword she twists and crinkles the napkin until it begins to flake apart on the table. Lost in its brown and yellow coffee stains she continues to fidget until the words begin to break loose.

"Um, I don't... it's—"

"Katrina, forget it. I didn't mean to make you uncomfortable, again." I interrupt.

"No, you deserve to know. Everything you did and what you said, everything was great. Nicer than anyone's been to me in a while." She sighs and takes a deep breath. "I suffer from delusions brought on by my brain cancer. Sometimes I hallucinate, when you were holding me, talking to me, I came to and saw my dad..." She trails off, tears gliding from her cheeks and peppering the tabletop. "He's dead." She sniffles, trying to suppress her tears.

I am such an asshole. Here I thought her problem was with me. All of this comes with the swift realization that not everything is about me. Lesson learned, but what the hell do you say to something like this?

"Thank you," I say, pushing her chin up with my index finger.

"Thank you?" she says, wiping her tears away with the bottom of her sleeve. "For what? Being a bitch to the only person who was trying to help me?"

"No, for sharing that with me." I smile. "Does the group day alternate every week?" I ask, changing the subject.

And with that, our conversation bursts forth like a river smashing through a dam. The emotional concrete walls smash to dust, we talk about everything. I tell her more about work, my friends and family, what movies I like. She goes on about meetings and treatment schedules and how the best thing about

29

having cancer means no longer having to work. Time is draining fast from the clock and we don't notice the attendant locking up. A 17-year-old-counter clerk comes over and politely tells us to get the fuck out. We take our endless conversation to the street, walking slow to prolong our night together. A few blocks away from Starbucks I light up a cigarette and she shoots me a nasty glare.

"What are you doing?"

"What? You're not going to let a man on death row smoke?"

"Stop it. That's not funny."

"Sorry." Taking a long hard drag I flick my half smoked cigarette into the street.

We walk another block silently enjoying each other's company before she stops and turns to me.

"I had a good time tonight, talking to you," she says smiling.

"Oh yeah, hey, me too. Thanks for giving me a chance."

"Well, you don't seem like much of a psycho," she laughs giving me a playful shove. "But if you want to do something like this again you have my number."

"Thanks. That would be great," I say, repressing any giddiness. One goodbye hug later and I head back my car.

I pull into my driveway after midnight, satisfied. Grandma was right. Get her out once and she's yours. Still sitting in my car I call work and talk with the night manager. By now word of me stroking out has reached him. He expresses his concern but I ease his mind by telling him it was the result of a longstanding bout with insomnia. I tell him the doctor said I should take the weekend off, knowing that my credibility is good and they won't ask for a doctor's note. I end the call and walk to the front door. On the step is a case of Coronas and a piece of paper is taped to my door. Fuck, I forgot about Nick. I kick the 12-pack, it's empty. I tear off the note; it says:

Where were you tonight? Waited three hours and drank all the beer. Could have let myself in but didn't. Would have called but forgot my phone. Call me in the morning. -Nick

Inside, the telephone begins ringing almost immediately. I run through scenarios in my head of what I'm going to tell Nick. How I'm going to explain blowing him off. Taking a deep, breath I answer.

"Hey man I'm real sorry."

"For what?" Katrina says in her most innocent sounding voice.

"Katrina? I'm sorry I thought you were someone else."

"Nope, it's just me. I wanted to give you a quick call to thank you. I haven't talked to someone like that in years. I mean, I've spent time with Sally and she might tell you we're friends, but not like that. That was relieving, to share with someone and actually feel them care."

31

I don't answer; thankfully she can't see my face flushing red. "Dave? You still there?"

"Yeah, sorry, you just caught me off guard. Well, I'm glad I could help. And if you ever need to call don't hesitate, I keep odd hours."

She giggles. "I may just take you up on that, I don't sleep well either."

After an hour, we hang up. I'm tired, no, exhausted, despite not having done anything today. Walking towards the bedroom I shed clothing throughout the apartment, leaving a trail right to bed. My lead eyelids shut seconds after hitting the pillow and finally, I sleep.

It was a restless night's sleep but better than anything since my diagnosis. My dreams plagued by abstract colors and shapes. I remember seeing Katrina's face; only she wasn't sick and had a head full of blonde hair. Then her face would melt into Nick's face and he would be yelling at me about ditching him. Then I would see myself, but I would look like I was 80 years old. This is why dreams are pointless. What's the use in fretting over unintelligible brain signals? If we were supposed to understand them we would.

I am sitting out on my back patio smoking again. It has been a slow Saturday with nothing to do. I fucking hate days like this, especially since my diagnosis. It's like I can feel the cellular decay sitting here doing little more than waiting to die. I go over last night in my head again and again hoping I said all the right things. Hoping I didn't offend her. Sometimes it seems like that's the only thing I am good at is offending people. And hating them.

My neighbor slides open his patio door with a thud and his border collie charges out. The collie goes through her normal ritual of running circles in their yard until she builds up enough speed to charge through the invisible fencing into my yard. She paces for a few more seconds, then poops. Every spring when the snow melts my backyard looks like an ill kept dog kennel. Small brown piles mining the entire yard. But it's only during the winter months. I watch as the dog does its business, finishing with a few kicks from her hind legs.

Then it hits me; I don't have any pets. I love dogs, cats, and most animals in general. But I live here, alone. I sit up in my chair to get a closer look at the dog and the sound of my feet scuffing the wood perks her ears up. I let out a slight whistle and the dog hesitantly approaches the deck. I walk down the wooden steps and halfway into the yard to greet her. She plops her butt down on the ground and cocks her head giving me the strangest look. I kneel, and read the engraved golden tag attached to her collar; Jenifer.

How peculiar, who gives a dog a persons name? Then suddenly the dog's name doesn't matter. The poop in my yard doesn't matter. The only thing that matters is that she's here with me right now. This small companion doesn't judge me for being sick or weak, or irresponsible. The only thing she wants is my attention.

"You're just a lonely sweetheart, aren't you girl?"

Her ears perk up again and she mashes her wet nose into my face and licks my mouth. Then she stops and puts her paw up in the air.

"You want to shake?" I say, taking her paw and introducing myself. "Names Dave, pleased to meet you, Jen."

"What the hell are you doing?" Nick laughs. He startles me and Jen, causing her to jump away and fly towards the backyard. "Did you get a dog?"

"No. She's my neighbors," I say, watching her dart through the invisible fence and wait at my neighbor's door.

My neighbor slides open the door and she charges in. He looks out across the backyard to me and Nick. I give him a friendly wave, but he just slams the door shut without any acknowledgement.

"What a dick," Nick says, shaking his head.

"I don't even know his name."

"Huh?"

"I've lived here for like seven years and I don't even know his name. It makes me feel like I've missed so much. What the hell have I been doing with my life?"

Nick looks at me, perplexed at this sudden flood of emotion.

"What's your point?" he asks.

"Nothing. Just thinking, it makes you wonder who the dick is."

"Stop man, you're cool. Communication works both ways, remember."

"Yeah, I guess."

"Come on; let's go get some food, and maybe a drink to help you forget about your new furry girlfriend." He laughs at his own joke.

Walking towards the door my phone buzzes in my pocket. Fishing it out I see that it's Katrina and pause. Nick gives me a look as I remain frozen with my phone in my hand.

"Oh, your other girlfriend, I forgot. Well are you going to answer it?" His words are tart with irritation.

"I really should take this," I say pressing the phone to my ear. I catch him rolling his eyes before stepping back out onto the deck. "Hello?"

"Watchya doing?" Kat asks, but then begins answering before I can say anything. "I know, you're coming to Starbucks to meet me for an afternoon vanilla latte." I look through the sliding glass door at Nick leaning on the counter. He is going to be pissed if I bail on happy hour. But what choice do I have?

"Sure."

"Yay! I'll see you in a few." She hangs up without saying good-bye.

Closing and locking the sliding glass door I draw some pictures in the condensation on it before turning to face Nick.

"You're not coming are you?"

"Nick, I'm still coming, but could we meet up a couple hours later?"

"No, that's fine man, I get it. Go out with your little chick, have a good time. No worries."

He pats me on the back and then I walk him out. I know he's pissed but he won't ever show it. I get changed and go meet Katrina.

The week went fast even though I didn't have much to do. My stroke out gibberish episode keeps me out of work for over a week. Days are spent lying on the couch talking on the phone with Katrina or waiting for Nick to come over. I still visit Grandma at the usual times on the usual days. Outside the temperature is rising. The subtle signs of spring dancing in the March air. Giant snow mounds left behind by plow trucks are now small mud specked globs. The streets glisten, slick with melted snow.

In the parking lot of the church, my car windows are rolled down as soft rain patters against the hood of the car. I arrived a half hour early, waiting for Katrina, but she must be downstairs already. It would be nice to walk in with her, the alcoholic's anonymous meeting mix up left me a bit scarred. I give up, slamming my car door as I head inside.

In the basement I grab a cup of coffee and say hi to a few of the other terminals. The setup is the same as the first night. I walk around the big circle of metal chairs, approaching the spot where Katrina sat last week. Then my blood turns to ice. Her chair is empty. I try to calm down, assuring myself that she is late. Ten slow minutes pass as I stare at her empty seat; this warm circle of people is cut open by one cold, empty, metal chair. I can't concentrate. Sally's words crackle unintelligibly like white noise. Twenty minutes pass, activities are set to begin. No Katrina. I'm sweating, what if she is dead? The empty metal folding chair mocks me. Tells me I never should have gotten close. A splitting migraine kicks in full force. Every sound in the room is amplified and distorted. Hearts pounding like bass drums, tapping pens firing like cannons, Sally's voice wails like an accordion. A man's coffee whooshes like a waterfall out of the pot and into his Styrofoam cup. At this point even the empty chair appears to be making noises. Is this me or my sickness? Overwhelmed I cover my ears and buckle forward, tears about to fall from my eyes and blood about to drain from my nose. Then a single voice shatters the sounds and everything stops.

"Are you okay Dave?" Sally asks.

I raise my head upright as my nose starts to gush. Sally puts her arm around me and asks if I'm okay again. My eyes dart around the room. Forty five minutes. No Katrina. I clutch my stomach and lower my head letting blood run down my face, chin and neck.

"Where's the bathroom? I'm going to be sick."

Sally helps me to the bathroom and returns to the group at my request. I splash myself with cold water, washing the blood off my face. Leaning forward, I lay my sweaty forehead on the cool edge of the large aluminum sink. I don't know if this is a panic attack because of Katrina's absence or because of my brain tumor. I walk over and lock the door to the single person bathroom. Sitting on the toilet I take out my cell phone and dial Kat. Six rings, voicemail. End call. Redial. Six rings, voicemail. Repeat. No answer. Voicemail. I cram my phone back into my pocket. The sick anxious feelings pass. Numbness washes over me. What if she is dead? What about our conversations? My feelings for her? None of that matters now. She was right; I shouldn't have become attached to her. With no real way of composing myself I set my phone ringer to vibrate and head out to face the group.

"Dave, how are you feeling?" Sally belts out as soon as I am in sight.

"What the fuck does it matter?" I say taking a seat in my metal chair, right next to the empty one.

"Okay, moving on." She says in her know-it-all nasal tone. "Our final exercise tonight is going to be a group exercise. We are going to explore the different ways we are living and coping with our disease. One at a time we will explain what our day is like, treatment schedule, group therapy, physical therapy, and whatever else our day may consist of. Does anyone want to volunteer to go first?"

An older man named Ray raises his hand and gets the go ahead from Sally to tell us his pathetic story. Ray, peach fuzz head and ratty Salvation Army clothes. You can never tell someone's age here because of the cancer. They could be 20 or 80. Poor nervous dying Ray. He is standing in the center of us, clearing his throat, and preparing to talk about his sad routine.

"Hi everybody…" That's all I hear. I close my eyes and lean my head back waiting for this guy to finish. Maybe I should get up and leave, never come back. These people can't help me, I can't even help myself.

"Dave, you look like you might be able to benefit from discussing your daily routines. Why don't you go next?" Sally says bringing me back.

"Where's Kat?" My words echo of off the basement walls, cutting a sharp slice of silence through the whispers and murmurs of the other patrons. Sally even takes a step back, as if those words mean anything to her.

"Katrina isn't present tonight Dave."

"Well, where is she? Did you call her?" As I look around the circle people look away. They stare at the floor or their laps, looking anywhere but in my eyes.

"Dave, not everyone can make it every week. Sometimes life gets in the way,"

"But did you even call?"

"Would you like to go next?" She ignores my question and it pushes me over the edge.

"So this is what you do? Pretend like they were never here and move on? Scan the obituaries and send some flowers to the family? Fine, whatever, I'll take my fucking turn! I spend my day's chain smoking, plotting out my suicide. And now I remember why, so I don't become like you people."

Before the shock wears off and anyone can react I storm up the cement steps and out to my car.

I wind my car through narrow one way streets no bigger than alleyways, taking the long way home. Sally is alerting the authorities to my suicidal behavior. Katrina is dead in her bed or on her bathroom floor. Another faceless cancer victim with no family. Found by police when a neighbor reports a foul smell from the apartment next door. I'll go home alone and try to sleep knowing I am going to die. Knowing I have a bomb within my head. I'll never go back to group. Sally will search the obituaries for my name and picture to see if I followed through. I don't feel anything. Not sad, angry, happy. Just, nothing. I feel empty. As empty as Katrina's seat. As empty as my life. I pull off to the side of the road and recline the driver's seat. I need a break. Maybe I'll sleep here; it's as good a place as any. I am staring at the black cloth ceiling when a small white light brightens the interior of my car. I pick up my phone off the passenger's seat and look at the Caller ID; unknown number.

"Hello?"

"Dave?" A soft voice says.

"Yeah. Who is this?" I say, not even paying attention, only half hearing the voice.

"It's me, Katrina. Oh, I'm so glad I remembered your number." Hearing her name, said in her voice, relaxes every muscle in my body. I sit straight up in my seat with renewed energy.

"What's up? You weren't at group tonight, is everything okay?" I ask, trying not to sound too worried.

"Yeah, I'm okay, but I need a favor from you," she says, breaking into a coughing fit. I wait for it to subside before speaking.

"Sure, whatever you need."

"Well, I had an episode. I'm being discharged from Nadurra General Hospital in a few minutes. I don't have anyone to come and get me ... I know they have volunteers who provide rides ... but I don't want to be alone when they leave. Would you be able to pick me up and hang out with me?"

"Of course," I say, already starting the car and buckling my seat belt.

"Thank you so much. Pull up to patient discharge and I'll be waiting inside."

We say good-bye and hang up. My headache is gone, which means it was stress. I can feel again and I feel elated. Something happened and she needed someone and she called me.

I drive up to patient discharge and see Kat sitting in a wheelchair behind the glass sliding doors. She looks like pulverized shit and is wrapped in a ton of blankets. I head inside as three EMT's are wheeling out this huge man on a gurney. He smiles at me and I return the gesture. I walk up and kneel eye to eye with Katrina.

"How ya feeling, killer?"

"I've been better," she sniffles, playing with a wrinkled tissue.

"Anything need to be signed or filled out or are you set?"

"I'm all set, get me out of here."

I roll her down the handicapped ramp to my car and open the passenger door. I return to her, putting my arms around her to help her up when I notice that she is crying and dabbing her eyes with the crinkled tissue.

"Hey, what's the matter?" I ask.

She hesitates, looking at her legs wrapped tightly in blankets. "I can't walk. It's because of the chemotherapy," she says through tears.

"Oh shit, fuck, I'm sorry. Here, wrap your arms around my neck," I say, lifting her up and carrying her to the passenger seat. I get her buckled in and take the driver's seat.

"Dave?" She sniffles.

"Yeah?"

"Thank you."

"Don't worry about it. You would have done the same for me. Now, how do we get to your apartment from here?"

As it turns out apartment was a poor choice of words. Katrina's condo is humongous. I carry her tiny frame up the elevator and over the threshold, my little corpse bride. I am taken aback. Shinning mahogany wood covers the floor of the spacious living room. Floor to ceiling glass windows look out over the city from the tenth floor. Not that it matters, but she must come from serious money to afford this without working. I kick my sneakers off at the door and carry her to the couch, laying her down as if I were tucking in a baby.

"You didn't have to take your shoes off."

"Sure, where can I find some blankets and pillows?"

"In the bedroom at the end of the hallway, on the left. Top shelf in my closet."

I make my way to her bedroom, admiring the array of contemporary artwork decorating the walls. A few minutes later and Kat is nestled snuggly on her fluffy white couch within piles of feather pillows and comforters.

"Is there anything else you need? Are you hungry?"

"Dave, you've done way too much. Come sit down."

"Come on Kat, you have to be hungry. Let me cook you some dinner. What are you craving?"

She pauses for minute and then smiles at me. "Macaroni and cheese."

"Done. It may take me a bit to get my bearings in your kitchen."

After about 40 minutes of her calling out locations and me making a mess of her gorgeous marble countertop I return to the living room with two bowls of macaroni and cheese.

"Thanks. Want to watch a movie?" She says, turning on the TV with the remote control. "I have a billion channels that I never watch."

"Sure," I say, chuckling to myself. It's strange but I get the feeling she hasn't had any company in quite a while. I squeeze on to a small portion of the couch, trying to allow enough room for her to stretch out.

After dinner I do the dishes and hear Katrina shut off the TV. I walk into the living room with the damp dishtowel slung over my shoulder. Kat is stretched out on the couch enveloped in blankets and pillows, staring at me with a giant smile.

"Are you okay? Do you need anything?" I ask, because right now, whether she realizes it or not, I would do anything for her.

"Come here."

Walking over to her the dishtowel falls off of my shoulder and slaps against the floor. The echo of the wet slap catches me off guard. This place is magnificent, spacious, and largely empty. There is an overwhelming sense of loneliness here. It's like there is no trace of her. No unopened mail, or pictures of family members. Not even a refrigerator magnet.

I kneel on the floor next to her and she reaches her hand off the couch placing it in mine. My warm and pruned dishwater logged hand. It catches me off guard but I do my best not to notice it.

"Thank you for this."

"Kat, I already told you not to worry about it," I pause looking down at our hands, "But now I need to ask you something, the same thing you asked me at the coffee shop." She cocks her head a little, waiting for me to continue. "Why did you call me? You could have called friends, or your family, why me?"

She sighs deeply, almost like she knew this was coming.

"I told you my dad passed away," she sniffles, trying to choke back a tear. "He was a helicopter pilot for the Air Force. His unit was shot down over Afghanistan six years ago."

"But he couldn't have been the only person in your life?"

"No, he wasn't. My mom got sick and passed away when I was really young, family curse," she taps the side of her head with her free hand. "We moved around so much I never knew the rest of my family. I made a few friends living in military housing, but my dad was constantly being shifted from base to base, so it was pretty much just the two of us. I'll never forget the day they brought his flag, all folded up," she trails off and I give her hand a squeeze. "After that I sold everything

I had and just kept moving. I only stopped here because I got sick."

What does someone even say to that? I look at my reflection in the gloss varnish of the floor trying to decide how to continue. If circumstances were different I would just kiss her right now. But this isn't exactly a normal first date. If you could call it a date. I glance up at her and see she is fast asleep. Her hand is gripping mine as if she never plans on letting go. I set the damp dishtowel onto the coffee table and lay my head on the edge of her pillow to rest my eyes for a bit. Unexpectedly I fall fast asleep, kneeling on the hardwood floor.

The smell of eggs, bacon, and dark toast stirs me from my sleep. I roll over squeezing the feather comforter tight against my chest. Stretching my limbs further than normal I realize this is way too big to be my bed. I open my eyes and am staring up at a perfect blue sky. Sun rays are shining through the large skylight windows above the bed, warming my face. This isn't my house. Looking underneath the blankets, I thank God that I am fully dressed. Sitting up, the bed is high enough that my feet dangle without touching the wood floor. On the nightstand are my cigarettes and wallet. I grab the cigarettes first and then pocket my wallet. Rubbing my eyes, I go into the kitchen following the home cooked smell.

"Hey sleepy." Katrina says, piling scrambled eggs on a plate with a spatula.

"Morning, you look better," I say, placing a cigarette between my lips.

"Yeah, I woke up a little wobbly but at least I can walk."

"You didn't have to make me breakfast. You should be resting."

She brings the plates over to the dining room table. "Hush now. Who says I am making you breakfast?"

"Well I figured, "

"Shh," she says with a smile. "I was hungry and made breakfast. I just happened to make enough for two."

"Thanks for including me. Where can I smoke?"

"If you must, smoke on the balcony. But here, take a glass of orange juice with you."

I go through the living room, my bare feet freezing on the wood floor. It had been so dark last night when we got home that I hadn't noticed the sliding glass doors. Outside on the balcony in the brisk morning air I light my cigarette. I don't remember how many floors up this is but it is high enough to give me vertigo. I sip my orange juice and admire the view. The one great thing about dying is the ability to stop and enjoy the moment. Katrina slides open the balcony door and stands in the doorway. I can feel her staring at me.

"Hey," she says. "I want thank you for last night. It's just, why did you help me? I was such a bitch to you."

"You're sick and got defensive. No big deal." Turning around, I lean on the rail. "But I didn't go to group to meet people. I went because I'm scared and sick, like you. Nobody understands what this is like, not my friends and not my family. But you're different. You're my age. We like the same things. But more important, we're losing the same things. I felt like I knew you the second I saw you."

"Wow, don't hold back," she says, laughing a little.

"We can't afford to hold back Kat. I think that is what I'm supposed to learn in all of this. It's like in the blink of an eye this will all be gone." I motion towards the city below us.

"Trust me, I know what you mean." She steps forward and leans her arms on the railing admiring the antlike people below. "I bet they all have no idea."

"No idea?"

"That we're up here dying together," she says.

8

I wake up to the telephone ringing, not an unusual event anymore. Groggy, I don't look at the clock, it's still dark out so I know it's early.

"Ugh, hello?"

"Hey, it's me," she says, way to perky for my taste, at least this early.

"Kat? It's like three in the morning, are you okay?"

"Oh yeah, I'm fine." And then silence, such a long pause the phone starts sliding down my face as I doze. "Do you want to get breakfast or lunch today?"

Of all the days she wants to hang out she picks today. The most important day since my diagnosis. Not sure what to do I take the first step towards what usually destroys my relationships; I lie to her.

"Kat, I'd love to but I have to work all day and then I'm having dinner with my parents." I throw in the dinner part to make it a half truth.

"Oh, it's okay. I just needed a ride to pick up some prescriptions."

"Kat, could we maybe do it tomorrow?"

"No, it's okay, I understand. I'll call Sally for a ride, she's helped me before. Sorry to bother you so early."

"No Kat, wait—"Dial tone. She always pops out as quickly as she pops in. I flip my phone to silent and roll over to go back to sleep. Sometimes it's easier to run damage control than tell the truth. But for now I need to rest up for my big day.

9

Wake up early, shower, and have a big breakfast. I called off work the night before so I could get extra sleep. When I finally leave the house it's raining. Raining hard. As I visit various gun shops around the city the pouring rain beats harder and harder against my car. It would seem God has conspired with Mother Nature to foil my plot of self-destruction. They underestimate my resolve; I meant what I said at group.

All the stops prior were pointless. Cramped stores with small selections. But not this one. When I step through the large glass doors I am immediately taken aback. Rows of shotguns border the walls. Every kind you could possibly imagine from jet black pump-actions still shimmering with a fresh coat of grease, to rusted out wood gripped double barrels taken in on consignment. The center of the selling floor is a labyrinth of racks jam packed with rifles. Sniper rifles with scopes, AR-15 assault models, and bolt-action .22's. Below each rack, stacked neatly, is the corresponding ammunition. I have never actually seen a gun or bullet aside from the movies. And now I stand before this great behemoth, a venerable Toys

"R"-Us of weapons. Before I can catch my breath, an older salesman calls out to me from behind a long glass counter, offering his years of experience. If he only knew my intentions.

This single thought stops me, because suddenly I'm not even sure of my intentions. I tell him I'm just browsing and begin to stalk the racks, brushing my fingertips over the waves of armament. Suicide. The ultimate show stopper. So dramatic, I don't even know if this is me or my rotten brain. I can see, even hear the people that I love in my head. My parents, grandparents, Nick. Words like coward and quitter pour from their mouths. But that's not it, I know it isn't. Because along side of the people I love I can see people from the group. Rows of sad, gaunt faces. Sunken eyes and bald heads. Bones ready to tear through paper-thin skin. That's when I remember what I'm in for and that's when I'm certain. This isn't an act of fear; it's an act of courage. When my body deteriorates enough, becoming a prison, the gun will be the key. It can stop this disease. The bullet is my cure. I shut my eyes tight for a quick second, and the only person left in my head is Katrina. A single reason to endure. A beautiful soul, etched in the darkness of my mind, pleading with her eyes for me to reconsider. But is it enough? I weave my way back to the salesman and tell him what I'm looking for, credit card in hand.

And now, not but an hour later, I sit alone in my living room with the gun reflecting in the glass coffee table in front of me. It was that easy. A new shotgun that still has the glossy coating of unsullied wood and untarnished metal. A gun that has never taken a life will start by taking mine. Lifting the gun I look down the iron sights, feeling its thick dead weight in my hands. Time to rehearse. I push the barrel underneath my chin. It's not comfortable. There's no point in holding it to my temple; it's way too long for that. But I had this in mind when I bought it. I reach into the plastic bag by the foot of the couch. I take out the new hack saw and pull the tags off.

Then, alone on my couch, I do what only the movies could have taught me. Sawing the wooden end of the stock off, I create a crude pistol grip. Then, like I know what I'm doing, I pick an arbitrary spot near the end of the fore grip and saw most of the barrel off. It's become is a powerful little tool, maneuverable enough to paint either the ceiling or wall with my cancer-ridden brains. The truth is, I don't know if it's going to blow my head or my hand off. I can only hope for the latter. I lift the sawed-off shotgun to my temple. It's do-able but still cumbersome. I put the barrel in my mouth and wrap my lips around the rough cut edges. Then I think that maybe I don't want the last thing I taste to be burning sulfur. I would point it at my heart but that seems less than instant, what if I miss? Then it strikes me that I shouldn't put this much thought into it. Maybe some elements in my death should be a surprise.

I set the gun on the table; my hand is shaking. This is the closest to death I have ever been. It's a mind fuck, having a gun in your mouth. Picking up my new piece I move to my bedroom. Passing the large mirror on the closet door, I catch a glimpse of myself. I pause and strike a quick pose, looking pretty badass with a gun. On a whim I put the barrel under my chin and stare for a second. My heart races. I walk to my dresser and stuff the gun in the sock drawer. It's getting late and I have to meet my parents at my grandparent's for supper.

I hate spaghetti and meatballs, not that it's bad food, on the contrary. When my mom teams up her cooking skills with my grandma's off-the-boat Italian meatball-making-skills, the food is quite decadent. But growing up, this was a daily meal, sometimes more if you count leftovers, so it's not my favorite. Then a flash inside my head, a picture of what awaits me, what's hiding in my apartment in the depths of my sock drawer, and suddenly the idea of spaghetti and meatballs doesn't sound so bad. But the mood here is tense, it stems from the everlasting conflict of two women trying to outdo each other's cooking. The air in the kitchen is thick with the odor of homemade sauce and old coffee. Standing at the counter with an empty plate in my hand I can hear my stomach growling over my grandpa's blaring television. My mom takes the empty plate, filling it with a mountainous portion of spaghetti, but only one meatball. What the fuck? I hold my plate out in front of me staring at the lone meatball.

"So, about that one meatball, mom."

"Stop, just because you've grown up and moved out doesn't mean the rules change. Kids get one, wives get two, and husbands get three. Maybe you should become a husband if you want more meatballs," she says.

Taking a seat at the kitchen table, I say, "I'll keep that in mind."

Now one thing about my grandma is that she loves gossip. I really used to hate that about her. But after today, I imagine how painfully ordinary my life would have been without it. Some of the deepest conversations we've had started out with some sordid rumor about the neighbors. And then it occurs to me, it was never really about the gossip, it was about me listening to her. Being there when no one else would find the time. And then there is a pain deep inside my chest, where I can feel the emptiness my absence will bring to her life.

"Have you told your parents about that nice young girl you met?" Grandma says with a smirk before sipping her glass of water.

I stay quiet, twirling my fork in my spaghetti spoon and thinking of how to continue. Not even upset that this time the gossip is my own.

"Why no, he hasn't. Where did you meet her?" my mom asks.

"It's complicated, and we're not serious, just friends," I say skirting the question.

My phone starts ringing, saving me from an already uncomfortable conversation. I look at the Caller ID, it's Kat, thank God. I stand, giving my family a sheepish grin.

"I have to take this, it's work." I say, walking out onto the porch.

"Sure it is." I hear my grandma say before closing the front door behind me.

"What's up?" I ask, pressing the phone to my ear.

"I don't care where you are right now. You need to come home."

After giving Kat my address and telling her where the spare key is, I say a hasty goodbye and take a large Tupperware container of food. Katrina is already at my house when I arrive. The living room lights are cutting a beam through the night as I pull into the driveway. I'm barely through the door and she's in my face.

"Sally shared some concerns about you on the way to the pharmacy," she says, her arms crossed. "She told me what you said."

"Told you what?"

"Admit it. You know what I'm talking about." She starts tapping her index finger on her elbow. I stare with a blank face not sure where she is going with this. "You're not going to get treatment? Suicide? You really know how to make someone feel special.   Have you lost your fucking mind?"

She is screaming and ramming her finger into my chest. This is the first time she has ever sworn around me.

"Back off. It's none of your business. Besides look at what that shit is doing to you, it's killing you."

"No, it's not, Dave. It's curing me," she says. "And, not my business?"

"Curing you at what cost Kat? Look at you, you look like a corpse!"

"What do you mean it's none of my business?"

"It's not like you're going to be around to see me go anyway. What does it matter if I put a gun in my mouth?"

"Do you hear yourself? If you really meant this, why would you have come to group? And besides what if it's you?" she asks.

"What if what's me?"

"The cure. What if your unstudied, undocumented version of our disease holds the cure that could save us or everyone else? You selfish prick."

"I don't want to live this way Kat. Waiting for you to die and then waiting for me to die. I want to experience life. I want to switch it all into fast-forward. Live an entire lifetime in an instant. Is that wrong?"

"Live an entire life in an instant? You can't have both. Who are you lying to Dave? Me, group, or yourself?"

I turn away and begin playing with the curtains, staring into the night. She's right, who am I lying to? I bought a gun, but not because I want to use it. Not right now at least. The gun is a contingency plan. My own personal Jack Kevorkian, living in my sock drawer, for when my health turns to shit. But I can't argue anymore. The reason I didn't tell anybody was because of this moment. I don't want to hurt anyone, and now I see that is impossible. But I have a choice; I can be the bad guy, or this disease can be the bad guy. I grab my coat from the dining room chair and start towards the door and slide a cigarette between my lips.

"You would really kill yourself?"

"Kat, I don't know."

I open the door and look out into a night so dark it could swallow me whole, if only it would. "Lock up when you leave." Lighting my cigarette, I slam the front door. It's better this way.

Three hours later I return home. I turn the key to unlock the dead bolt but it's not locked. Opening the door I tiptoe into the living room. Katrina is lying on the couch wrapped in blankets and pillows from my bed, fast asleep. The sight of her stops me. What am I doing? I've been in love with this girl since I first saw her. Even after she rejected me I knew that eventually she would let me in. Now she's crashed on my couch, after I was such a bastard. Who tells the person they love they're going to kill themselves? Me.

I slip my shoes off and glide across the floor in my socks, squatting next to her, and run my hand down her cheek. A single, miniscule tear forces its way out of my tear duct. She came here trying to save me. I am a bastard, but this is where it ends. I tried to help her and she rejected me, now she's tried to help me and I rejected her. If I really love her, this deserves a fresh start.

I squeeze on a sliver of space behind her on the narrow couch and wrap my arms around her. She stirs in her sleep from my touch.

"You're still here," I whisper into her ear.

"Yeah, guess I am," she says in a soft sleepy voice.

"Kat, I want to…"

"Shh, we can talk in the morning," she interrupts.

I squeeze her tight and close my eyes. And for the first time in a long time I fall into a deep restful sleep.

When I wake up Katrina's gone, guess she changed her mind. I slept late, it's already noon. That's when I hear the sound of plates and chairs being moved about in the kitchen. Further investigation reveals Katrina sitting at the kitchen table with lunch. She has a notepad and a pen next to her plate. She smiles big when she sees me. She doesn't look bothered by what happened last night.

"Morning sleepy. Come sit, I made lunch for us," she says. "And, we need to talk."

I scratch the dry itchy scalp of my unwashed bed head and take the seat across from her. I can't imagine what it says in that notebook.

"Well?" I say, lifting my sandwich for a bite.

"You want to live it up? Do as much as you can as fast as you can? Prove it," she says, flopping down her notepad beside my plate. I stare at it, a half-chewed bite of roast beef sandwich hanging out of my mouth.

She continues, "You're right, we don't have much time left. Days, weeks, months. Who knows? We need to start living. Now I know you hate Sally and her bullshit but she gave me an idea awhile ago. We're making a bucket list and following through with everything on it." She stops talking and starts eating her sandwich, waiting for my response.

"Okay." I say, still not finished chewing.

"Okay? That's it?"

"Yeah, when do we start?"

"Tomorrow. Today we plan."

Sticks and twigs crackle under our feet, echoing in the quiet of our morning trek. Katrina keeps a tight grip on my arm and I walk slowly to compensate for her frailty.

"Where are we going?"

"I told you it's a surprise," I say.

A squirrel scampers in front of us and scurries up an oak tree. Kat stops walking for a second and looks around. The woods are still dark and everything has a creepy blue tint. It's hard to see anything in this dim lighting. Every small rustle of leaves or sticks sounds like a wild animal readying an attack. I slide my arm out of her grip and put it around her.

"Are you okay? Do we need to turn back?" I ask.

"No I'm fine. I've never been in the woods at night, it's scary, but I want to take it all in."

"Don't think of it as night, it's less scary if you look at it as early morning," I say. She smiles at that thought and we continue.

The dense thicket of pine trees opens up, revealing a small clearing. The crunchy carpet of dead pine needles is replaced by thick grass shimmering emerald under a blanket of morning dew. In the center of the clearing is a dried-out log I dragged here when I was still in high school. This is my quiet place, perched high above the town I grew up in, overlooking the enticing glow of the city. As a kid I would sneak out to spend long nights here, staring out at the stars, and dreaming of living in the city. As I help her sit on the log, Katrina's mouth hangs wide when she peers over the edge to see how high we are.

"Wow, this is, beautiful," she says.

We're so high up everything looks fake. A model world built in the basement of a toy train enthusiast. And the silence. No noises of honking horns, or rumbling motorcycles. Not even the sound of a passing plane. Just the peace and quiet of a toy world, veiled in the blue-grey haze of the morning twilight.

"When I was a kid, I used to come up here to think. I have only ever brought one other person up here," I say, thinking of Nick.

"Well I guess this makes me the second luckiest girl in the world."

"It wasn't a girl," I say. "Now, shush, it's time."

A reddish glow of orange pours over the horizon, illuminating the sky and turning the clouds into a tie-dye pattern of purple, pink, yellow, orange, and deep red. The colors wipe out the blue haze as sunlight washes over the entire land. First the city's landscape casts shadows of the massive buildings over the tops of the trees before us. The sun crests the top of the horizon, and burning bright, chases the rest of the darkness to the other side of the planet. It only lasts a few seconds, but we sit for a moment, letting the sun warm our faces. Katrina rests her head against my shoulder. I can feel her smile without needing to see it.

"You said you wanted to enjoy every sunrise. What better time to start than the day after we decided to start living?"

She says nothing in response, just intertwines her arm around mine and holds my hand. It solidifies what I felt the moment I saw her. This is true love.

Weeks pass by much quicker now. Our days overflow with the things we have always wanted to do. My biweekly visits to my grandparents become weekly visits. My drinking binges with Nick also have taken a back seat. Honestly, it's hard to even answer a phone call from him. I'm starting to think Kat is right and I am lying to myself. At first I didn't want to tell anyone about my disease because I needed time to let it sink in. It was hard enough to cope with it myself, let along cope with my family's reaction. Then it started to feel like something I had to hide, a weakness. Me and my rotten brain. Now that that pity-party is over, I am realizing it might just be cowardice, or selfishness. My inability to deal with the truth and the consequences it will bring. Sometimes my stomach hurts just thinking about it, even though the longer I wait the harder it will be. To ease my mind when it becomes overwhelming I try and focus on the moment. Summer has hit and the weather is beautiful. Blistering hot days are followed by warm nights. The extra daylight adds more time for us to spend together. We're both finally living our short lives to their fullest.

The repetitious clack of the roller coaster car mocks me as it makes its way up the steep incline. Suddenly, we're flat against our backs in the car as we ascend. My eyes are squeezed shut so tight it hurts. Inside, my breakfast churns into steaming vomit, waiting to eject from my belly.

"I can't believe you talked me into this," I say, keeping my eyes shut.

"You said you wanted to ride every ride. Well, open your eyes!" Her soft hand slides into mine and as our fingers interlace she squeezes. "Please, for me?"

Reluctantly, I open my eyes and become more disgusted. I can see everything I've never wanted to from up here. Tiny cars parked by ant-like people, the bird shit covered roofs of all the little gaming booths, dumpsters the size of Lego blocks, everything.

As we crest the peak the car's chain clacks one last time before releasing and we begin our rapid descent. I open my mouth to say something to Katrina but nothing comes out. On the way down wind tears at my face and hair. The sheer power of gravity forces me against my seat. A cacophony of screaming kids surrounds us. I fight to turn my head and look at Kat. She's relaxed, laughing. We continue our journey through big loops, upside down and then into a pitch-black tunnel. As soon as we enter the tunnel we're rocketing out the other side like childbirth at light speed. Then the screeching metal of breaks and we all jerk forward. When we stop and the noise is over I realize something terrible and embarrassing; I am the only one still screaming.

My screaming subsides and Katrina leans into me close and whispers into my ear, "You can let go of my hand now, we have to get off."

I loosen my rigor mortise grip and she pulls her hand back waving it in the air. There are deep purple finger dents along the back of her hand.

"Wow, I thought it was broken for a minute," she says. "Alright now we have to get off the ride."

She gives me a playful shove as the people waiting to get on grow audibly impatient. In a dazed state of shock I get off the ride, staggering to the left and right and stumbling towards a waist-high fence. My body crashes into the short chain-links with such force that for a moment I think I'm going right over. Before I can catch my footing breakfast makes its second debut of the day. The contents of my stomach propel outward, clearing a small embankment and flopping into the water of a log flume ride. For a moment I lay draped over the fence staring at my mess. The thickening remains of sausage gravy, scrambled eggs, biscuits, and coke floating in the river. I collapse to the ground lying with my back against a fencepost; sweaty, exhausted, and defeated by a kids ride. Kat kneels, putting her hand on my left thigh.

"You feeling okay buddy?" she says, with a gratified smile.

"My head hurts," I mutter with my eyes still closed.

"Well, if that's all we should get going."

"What's the hurry?" I choke out, followed by a quick gagging dry heave.

"Well, when that family of four came down the log flume ride, it threw your giant pile of puke everywhere, on them, the worker at the bottom, everywhere. And I heard them call for cleanup and security when the dad started yelling."

"I don't give a shit." I shut my eyes and lean my head into her chest.

"Well, that's unfortunate because I do," she says, pulling me to my feet and dragging me to the exit.

My cell phone vibrates in my pocket as she tugs me across the parking lot. I pull it out and see it's Nick. Without hesitating I shove it back into my pocket.

"Who is it?" Kat asks.

"Nobody, doesn't matter."

"Dave, you can tell me." We stop walking and she let's go of my hand. "Who is it?"

"It's my friend Nick."

69

"Answer it then, don't let me stop you."

"Kat, it's not you," I look at the phone as it stops vibrating, and then back to her. "I still haven't told anyone about my cancer."

A car passes by us kicking up a cloud of dust from the ground of the dirt parking lot. She doesn't say anything, just stares at me under the hot, setting sun. She comes closer to me taking both of my hands in hers.

"It's not something you should be ashamed of. I think you'd be surprised at the reactions you will get."

"I know, it's not that, I just, I don't know..." I look at the ground.

"Dave, when I was diagnosed I didn't have anybody to tell. You don't have to bare this burden alone, but you choose to?"

"I—"

"It's okay," she puts her hand on my cheek. "You'll tell them when you're ready."

Later that night we walk down the steps into the damp church basement carrying our own coffees. When we walk in together laughing and sipping drinks from the same place it raises a few eyebrows. Sally gives us the stare of death as we take our metal seats in the circle. The last few stragglers fill in the remaining empty seats and Sally takes her spot at the center of the circle.

"Today's activity is going to be a little different than usual," she says. Katrina and I keep talking as if Sally is invisible. "Dave and Katrina, is there something you would like to share before we begin?" She stops and stares at us.

I clear my throat. "No m'am."

"Well, let us continue then. Today we are each going to discuss one thing we have lost in our lives since our diagnosis. Something taken that we want back. Take a moment to think about the question and then whoever wants to go first can come to the center and lead us."

It doesn't take long for someone to stand up since we are all pretty pissed off and feel cheated out of a life. It's weird to think that every single one of us has been robbed of something we hold dear. The first person to take the center is poor old Ray. Ray with his broken life and his decaying body. He steps to the center and clears his throat.

"If I had to pick one, oh hell, I don't know there are so many. After my wife found out I was terminal she left me," he says, shifting nervously from foot to foot. "I guess she couldn't stand the thought of me dying. I don't know. Maybe she was looking for a way out …"

Ray bursts into melancholy hysterics. When I joined, Katrina was first in line for the abyss. Everyone was convinced she would be the first to die. But now Ray's health has taken a turn for the worse. His weight has been declining, his skin growing tight, his eyes sinking into his skull. He looks like hell, like he is already dead.

"I want my wife back ..." he manages to choke out between sobs.

"It's okay Ray," Sally says, stepping to the center of the circle to console him.

"That's all." His head dips down and he looks faint.

Sally puts his arm around her, wearing him like a rich woman would wear a fur mink. She gingerly wisps his frail body back to his seat. I turn to see Kat's reaction but to my surprise she is already heading toward the center of the circle with red puffy eyes. I thought I knew what words were going to come out of her mouth but nothing could have prepared me for what came next.

"I want to be beautiful again," she sobs. "I miss having long hair to comb. I miss having boobs. I'm so skinny. I miss it all." She lifts her t-shirt up to the bottom of her bra. "I can see my rib cage, and these bruises, this isn't beauty. I'm a monster."

Her breathing becomes heavier and more rapid. Losing her composure, she is overcome by a wave of tears and almost collapses. I walk to the center of the circle and put my arm around her.

"That's enough," I say, leading her away from the crowd. Sally waddles as fast as she can to keep pace with us.

"No, this is healthy, Dave. Let her continue."

72

"No. She's been through enough, she doesn't need this shit." I guide Kat up the stairs to get some fresh air.

The second we get outside Katrina turns and buries her face in my chest, crying harder than I've ever seen anyone cry before. Her tears are cool compared to the heat coming off her face and they soak through my shirt. I keep holding her and let her get it all out. She lifts her head and snorts up a loose line of snot before wiping her eyes.

"Thanks."

"Feel better?"

"No," she laughs through the tears.

"I know it won't matter if I tell you you're beautiful."

"You're right. But sometimes it's nice to hear," she says, blowing her nose on a tissue retrieved from her small purse.

"Let's go home, beautiful."

"What about group?"

"Fuck Sally. We'll catch them next week. Besides you've got treatment all day tomorrow and you need some sleep."

I pull out my keys and start towards the car when she wraps her arms around me. Before I can turn around she is giving me a giant hug, burying her face in my back. Wiggling around, I give her a tight squeeze and hold her.

Passing through the pharmaceutical section Kat picks up a box of nicotine patches.

"What are those for?"

"I just thought, you know,"

"Don't hold your breath." I scoff.

Reaching to the top of the white shelf I pluck off a pink package of adult diapers and drop them into the cart. As we round the corner into the magazine section Katrina places a craft magazine back onto the rack.

"Okay, you got me, why are we shopping in this tiny grocery store so far away from the city? And why are you buying adult diapers?"

"Well Kat here's the thing—"

"Prune juice, glucose test strips, fruit..." She continues to list off the weird items inside my shopping cart.

"Once a week I—"

"Instant coffee, Preparation H ..."

"Katrina, Focus."

"Sorry."

"Once or twice a week I visit my grandma. And grocery shop for her and my grandpa."

"You're introducing me?" I can see the excitement sparkling in her eyes.

"Yes."

"Well come on let's get going!" She jumps on the cart riding it to the end of the aisle like a little kid.

The sun warms us as we pull into my grandparent's driveway later that afternoon. I can see my grandma looking out the window trying to get a peek at who is there. Her fat Siamese cat is asleep on the window ledge. I put my hand on Kat's leg before she gets out of the car.

"Hey, I need something ..."

"What is it"?

"I haven't told anyone I'm sick. I don't know what it would do to Gram if she knew she might outlive me."

"What about your parents?"

"Nope."

"Nick?"

"Nobody. And I need you to keep my secret."

She smiles, takes my hand off her leg, and places it on the stick shift.

"Sure. I'll just add it to the list of things that I don't approve of."

Inside the kitchen Grandma greets us, oxygen tank in tow. However excited she was in the grocery store Katrina is now that much more terrified. She stands so close to my back, she is almost completely hidden behind me. Setting down the grocery bags on the counter I hug my grandma, knowing she will stare over my shoulder at Kat.

"Are you going to introduce me to your friend David?"

"Oh sorry Grandma, this is Katrina."

"What a beautiful name. Nice to meet you Katrina. Just call me Grandma, everybody else does." She smiles at Kat and delicately shakes her hand.

"Pleased to meet you as well ma'am."

"Oh, and manners too. David, this one might be a keeper." Katrina gives me a red-faced smile.

"Grandma!" I snap, my face flushing bright red.

"I'm sorry, but you know how us old people can be. I didn't mean to embarrass you two. Come and sit, it has been forever since you've visited."

She pulls her oxygen tank behind her and has a seat at the kitchen table.

"Actually, Grandma we are just stopping in to drop off some groceries."

"Oh don't leave. You two want to play a quick game of scrabble right?"

"Grandma, we've been out all night and most of the day and we're really tired."

"Oh come on, we have time for one game right?" Katrina says, tugging on my sleeve.

"It's settled then. I'll put on some coffee. David, get the Scrabble board, "Grandma says, ignoring my pleas.

13

I jolt awake sweating profusely at the kitchen table in front of the Scrabble board. I lose my coordination and tip out of my seat and onto the floor. To my left is Katrina, about to lay down some tiles. To my right is my grandma, sipping some coffee. They both jump from their seats as I fall. Kat grabs my hand putting her arm around me and helping me back up.

"Are you alright? You must've dozed off during the game," she says, looking concerned and trying to cover for me.

"I'll make him some tea." Grandma says, moving to the stove and flicking on the burner beneath a tea kettle.

"I don't drink tea, Gram ... and anyways I'm fine."

"Did you have a bad dream?" Kat asks, taking her seat.

"I ... don't remember. The last thing I remember was hoping you didn't use the triple word score because I had a great word."

She looks at my tiles and then back at me confused. "You have all vowels. And there's no triple word score left. Are you okay?"

I look at my Scrabble pieces. Nothing but vowels, no words. None of this makes any sense, it's like someone kicked the power cord out of the back of my brain. I stand, wobbly and nauseas, then take a sip of cold coffee. But my fingers don't want to listen to my brain and I drop the mug. The blue ceramic mug shatters against the linoleum floor. Katrina gets some paper towels from the counter and starts cleaning it up.

"Grandma, I don't feel too hot, I think we should go."

She stops making tea and comes over and gives me a big goodbye hug.

"I'm sorry," I say.

"Don't be, it was a pleasure meeting your new friend." She makes air quotes when she says the word friend. "Now go get some sleep. And don't be such a stranger."

Katrina gets in the driver's seat, demanding the keys. She is panicky so I hand them over without any fight. I light a cigarette and rub my face with my hands for a minute. It's like I can't wake up. I taste blood in the back of my throat and look in the mirror to see a tiny bit of dried blood crusted around my left nostril. My head hurts.

"What the fuck happened to me in there?" I ask, slapping myself on the cheeks.

"We need to get you to a hospital."

"No, just tell me what happened, please."

"You talked a bunch of gibberish and had a seizure. I told your grandma you do that when you're tired. Then I had to talk to her, ignoring that you could have been having an aneurism. Your nose also bled and you woke up freaking out. We need to get you checked out."

"No. Take me home. I just need some Advil and a nap."

"Seriously? And what if that happened while you were driving?"

"Please Kat, take me home."

"I can't drive; they took my license because I have seizures. You know that."

"Then why did you demand the keys?"

"I wanted to stop you."

We switch seats and leave my grandparent's house. Riding together in silence for nearly 15 minutes, I can tell she is pissed. But not pissed that I did something wrong, pissed because she is worried. I lean my right elbow on the center console resting my hand on the shifter. She takes me by the hand, willing me to look at her.

"I just want to help you." She locks her fingers into mine.

"I know; it's starting to sound familiar."

I drive to Katrina's apartment at 10:00 p.m. with a backseat full of surprises. As I pass the bus stop, I see her walking to her apartment. I slow the car down, put my four ways on, and pull up alongside her.

"Hey little girl, want some candy?"

She looks at me, startled at first, and then starts to laugh.

"What are you doing?"

"Get in I have a surprise for you."

"Dave, I'm tired, they kept me waiting forever at the hospital and I need to get some sleep."

"Kat, what did we talk about sleep?"

"I know, I can sleep when I'm dead."

"Good, get in."

"Fine."

She puts her hand on the door handle then looks in the backseat noticing the array of items. Two folding lounge chairs, a green and white flannel comforter, a cooler and a picnic basket.

"What do you have planned?"

"I guess you could call it a picnic," I say with a smirk.

"It's ten o'clock at night, I'm exhausted, and you want me to go on a picnic?"

"Yeah."

"Well, how can I resist?" She smiles and gets in.

An hour later we're sitting in our lounge chairs, listening to classical music and staring at the crisp night sky from the top of a parking garage. I take a bite of my sandwich and get lost staring into outer space.

"Kat, if you could have one thing before you die, anything, what would it be?"

"That's easy; I would want to be beautiful again."

"You're right, that is easy."

"Stop it, that's not what I meant. I want to look nice, like before I got sick. Before chemotherapy, like what I talked about in group. Sometimes in the morning I stare in the mirror trying to remember what my body used to look like."

"Like you looked before you stopped caring?"

Her head snaps to the right and two fiery eyes glare at me.

"That wasn't what I meant," I say. "I'm sorry. It's like when people are sick and get this death sentence they give up. And I don't understand it, when I found out I was going to die in a couple years, it made me want to live harder and faster than ever. Kat, I saw what you used to look like in the pictures around your apartment. You looked like Marilyn Monroe, and you still could."

Kat stares at her paper plate, a tear creeping down her cheek. Reaching over I wipe it off and take her hand.

"Hey, I didn't mean it like that. What I am trying to say is that you are beautiful. Don't cry—"

"I'm crying because I know you're right." She smiles at me and gives my hand a squeeze. "When I found out I had cancer I did give up. My family is gone and the only friends I had from work disappeared when the job did. Then, I saw the people at group, so sad and beaten down. I quit. It's too hard to go on without anybody in your corner."

"Well, you've got me now," I say, patting her hand. "But I do have to interrupt. It's getting close to midnight."

She dries her eyes on her sleeve as we stand. I help her to the concrete edge of the parking garage. With little effort I hoist her dainty frame onto the ledge and then hop up after her. She looks down at the city eight stories below.

"We're really high up."

"Hush, look over there towards the city. Three, two, one, wait for it …"

The darkness is shattered by an explosion of light from the top of the tallest building. Flowers of color burst in the sky over the city, mortars hiss and then boom exploding into showers and rainbow sparkles. Katrina sits at the edge kicking her feet like a little kid. She never takes her eyes off the sky

83

and I never take my eyes off her. The smile lines in her face from her huge grin. I watch the reflection of the fireworks bursting in her blue eyes. A few minutes later the commotion is over. In the distance police sirens flare up racing towards the building. Tomorrow this will make great headlines in the paper.

"How did you do that?"

"I paid some kids to light them off the top of the Parker-Morris building. Happy early birthday, Kat."

After all the time we spend gazing into each other's eyes, it only takes a second. I don't know what was said or what led up to it. One second we are holding hands walking to the door of her apartment on a warm summer night. Not five minutes later we are holding each other in a tender embrace. She peels off my black t-shirt and casts it to the floor. Kat runs her soft hands up my chest and then around the back of my neck. She pulls me in for another kiss. Then without any hesitation she takes her own shirt off. Still kissing her, I unsnap her bra and it falls to the floor. Her actions tell me she has no inhibitions left. No worries of my judgment about any part of her physical appearance. Her tiny bone white anorexic frame is speckled with a collage of freckles, chemotherapy burns, and sores. It takes a great amount of care not to hurt her. Feeling her wince as my hands graze a rough spot, I reposition them just below the contours of her rib cage. She's still wearing her blue do-rag with white clouds. Here in bed with

84

her hot naked body pressed into mine and her eyes closed she is as beautiful as the day they diagnosed her with cancer. We spend the rest of the night making love. Not fooling around or having sex, making love.

The red glow of the digital clock on her nightstand says 6:00 a. m. I have been awake a half hour. Katrina is nestled snug in my arms, out cold. I lie here, holding her and enjoying the moment, wishing it could last forever.

An hour later I slide my arm out from underneath her and grab my cigarettes off the nightstand. I look at the half-full pack in my hand and then look back at her sweet and peaceful in her bed. I walk across the large bedroom and into her bathroom, picking up my black t-shirt on the way. Turning the lights on, I open the medicine cabinet and take out the small box of nicotine patches. I set the box of patches on the counter and open my cigarettes. I take a big whiff of the tobacco smell emanating from the box.

"Well guys, we've had a good run. But maybe this will give me a little bit longer with her. I'll think of you when I'm drunk."

And with that, I turn the pack over, dumping the rest of my cigarettes into the toilet.

"Good-bye," I say crushing the empty pack and dropping it in after them. I flush the toilet and send them straight to hell.

I slide out a small patch and stick it to my bicep,

turning to see myself in the mirror. I look foolish wearing nothing but a nicotine patch. I pull my black t-shirt over my head and go climb back into bed. My clumsy fumbling stirs Katrina in her sleep.

"Who were you talking to babe?"

"Nobody. Go back to sleep," I say, wrapping my arms around her.

"You put your shirt back on ... I like to touch your chest," She squeaks, smiling and snaking her arms up under my shirt around my back. "Goodnight."

"Goodnight," I say, kissing her on the forehead and then on the lips.

15

I couldn't tell you when it happened but at some point group stopped being about group and started being about me and Katrina. People began to look up to us. Week after week they flock to us at the coffee table and we take turns telling them of our weekly exploits. They begin to ignore Sally, turning to us for advice, and everyone's always complementing Kat on how well she looks. We became a beam of light shining bright in that dark basement. Sally hated it. She started giving lectures aimed squarely at us. She would spend entire meetings telling us of the dangers of co-dependency. Giving examples of the depression survivor's guilt can bring on. Shame, guilt, fear, suicide. She would say all of this while staring directly at me and Kat. Reminding us of the one thing we would never bring up with each other. That no matter what, one of us is going to die.

After this week's meeting Sally boars her way through the hugging masses to get to us. We both see her coming and try to put as many people between us and her as we can. But it does no good. Sally's fat hand clamps around my wrist, wrenching my arm around her, hugging me tight. Leaning in close, she whispers into my ear.

"I know you and Katrina rode together. I would like a word with both of you before you leave." I see Katrina smirking over her fat shoulder. What else can I say?

"Okay," I blurt, wincing as I say it.

When the final stragglers leave with their lukewarm coffee and stale doughnuts Sally pulls three chairs out of the empty circle and we sit. Dragging her chair out in front of ours she faces us with crossed arms. She has the look of a disapproving mother.

"I see what's going on here and I don't like it," she says, tapping a finger against her fat bicep. "This co-dependency that is developing is not healthy for either of you."

"Excuse me?" I bite my bottom lip so hard it almost bleeds.

"You heard me. What do you two hope to get out of this? Group is for coping with our disease, not for lonely singles."

"Our disease?" I ask. "You're not sick Sally, well, physically at least. You're fucking sick in the head though, being here every week spitting up your preachy bullshit the way you do."

"I'm doing my small part," she starts to say.

"Shut up! I'm not finished—"

"No, you shut up, Dave!" Sally's abrasiveness catches me off guard. She is no longer speaking as the overbearing maternal figure. "You show up here arrogant and angry, I get it. You feel cheated, fine. But don't take your pathetic life out on those who wish to help. You come in here and have the nerve to gang up on me? You haven't let Katrina say one word, shows how much you care. Why don't you let her speak for herself?"

"Gladly," I say, glancing at Kat. She smiles at me and her gorgeous blue eyes ignite into flames. Like a female wolf whose pack mate is being threatened she is ready for the throat. This should be good.

"Katrina, would you like to add anything?" A chunk of fat just beneath her elbow ripples like a metronome as she continues to tap her index finger. "Katrina, did you hear me?"

"Yes I heard you and we have all heard you for way too damn long! I'm sick of this holier than thou bullshit attitude of yours. You encourage love and happiness in group, but when two people find it you try everything to stop it. And I know why Sally, why you need us suffering. If we're at peace we don't need you, or this group." Kat's eyes narrow to slits and her fangs retract having spit the last of their venom. "Come on, we're leaving."

Sally looks at me and I shrug, stand up and follow Katrina up the stairs and out the door of the church for the last time. When we get outside she turns to me.

"I can't believe I said that to her!" She jumps into my arms giving me a huge hug.

Tonight we walk back to her place after group knowing it's our last time there. The only reason we'll ever come back is to pick up the car. We have more to offer each other than they have to offer us. On our way home we stop for coffee and then detour through the park. At the park center we pause to admire the stone angel fountain and she pops the question to me. It catches me off guard and I don't know how to react.

"Is there any chance you will change your mind?"

"About what?" I say.

"About killing yourself?"

"You remember that conversation?"

"Of course."

"What makes you think I was telling the truth?"

"Because you wouldn't lie to me, and you haven't answered the question. So I will ask again, are you still going to kill yourself?"

Silence. I say nothing for what feels like an eternity. I have thought about this every day since I was diagnosed. Originally I didn't have a whole lot to live for. No wife or kids, only a handful of friends and family. It would be easy to disappear. But I also said that before I was in love. Before I knew how love felt. This isn't the time to tell her though, I can't have her thinking she saved me. At least not yet.

"I don't know," I say, looking away.

"Oh." She takes a sip of her iced coffee.

She takes me by the hand and gives me a kiss on the cheek. I look into her eyes and pause for a minute before giving her a kiss that could have lasted forever. Nervous butterflies well up in my belly as we stand under the moon making out in front of the park statue. No, I hadn't been in love when I bought that gun.

In a blur, she comes running in, hands full of plastic shopping bags. Smiling, she charges past me and into my bathroom. The lock clicks as I walk up to the bathroom door.

"What's the big surprise?" I ask through the door.

"Hold on a second! Go wait in the living room."

"Fine."

I go into the living room and sit on my couch. No sooner do I hear the door to the bathroom open.

"Are you ready?" she asks from the other room.

"Yes."

My heart beats out of my chest as she walks in. Kat is wearing a white dress with a split up the center in a V that starts at her belly button and widens to just cover her breasts. On the top of her head, where her do-rag was, is a curly blonde wig. She is wearing elegant jewelry, right down to ivory high heels. She does a little twirl as she walks over to me.

"They didn't have an exact replica of the Marilyn Monroe dress I wanted, but I think I came close. Do you like it?"

"Kat, I don't know what to say …"

"Say you like it."

"I love it. You're stunning, but …"

She shoots me a quizzical look. "But what?"

"Close your eyes."

"What?"

"Close your eyes."

She closes her eyes and I dart over to my desk, grabbing a black marker. I give her a little black dot on her right cheek, completing her transformation. Gently, I take her by the shoulders and guide her to the mirror on the back of the bathroom door. Leaning in close I whisper in her ear, "Open your eyes." When she does I can see she is startled by her own beauty.

"I'm gorgeous," she says.

Katrina closes her eyes and leans back into me. Content in this moment, I wrap my arms tight around her. She lifts her head looking over her right shoulder, her face so close to mine our noses almost touch. Her breath is warm and sweet across my face. As our lips are about to meet, I hear the door to my apartment burst open. Startled, we fly apart as if caught making out by our parents, our faces bright red. I rush into the living room towards the commotion to find Nick.

"Hey man is everything okay? You scared the shit out of me," I say, walking over to him. He storms up to me like he is going to beat my ass.

"No, everything is not okay! You haven't answered or returned my phone calls for weeks. And now, I come over, and you don't answer your fucking door?" he yells. When I do get the privilege of talking to you I get, I'm busy. Now you tell me, Dave, what the hell is keeping you this busy?"

His face turns white and he trails off. I look over my shoulder and see Katrina standing in the bathroom doorway looking absolutely incredible. Nick leans in close to me lowering his yell to a whisper.

"Can we talk outside?"

"Yeah," I say, ushering him to the door. We get outside onto my front step and I close the door behind me.

"Who the hell is that?"

"That would be my girlfriend, Katrina."

"Oh, it's only your ..."He interrupts himself, processing the thought. "Girlfriend? Oh good, it's only your girlfriend, Katrina, dressed like Marilyn Monroe, standing in your apartment. Listen I don't know what weird fetish you have but you better tell me what the hell is going on!"

"She is ..."

The creak of the front door opening interrupts our childish bickering. Katrina leans out and after an awkward pause, she breaks the silence.

"I'm not causing a problem between the two of you, am I?"

"No, I'm the one who's being a dick. Baby, this is my best friend Nick. Nick this is Katrina."

"Nice to finally meet you, I've heard a lot."

"Wish I could say likewise," Nick growls and then looks at the floor. "I mean he hasn't told me much."

"Kat, I've been blowing him and my family off for you and Nick stopped by to express his distaste for my choice."

"Well David, that's not nice, now is it?" she says with a smirk, walking up to Nick. "Nick we are about to go out to dinner at Le Mousseu's. It would be great if you could join us."

"No, no I wouldn't want to impose on the two of you, and I'm not dressed for that nice of a place," he mutters, shoving his hands in his pockets and looking at the cracked sidewalk beneath his feet. "But Dave if you could, please call me tomorrow."

"Sure man." I give him a hug and he tells Kat it was great meeting her and then leaves.

"Why did you invite him?"

"I had to save you somehow," she laughs as she walks toward my car.

I should have noticed the signs. Not long after we began living instead of just surviving, Kat began to get some color to her pasty white skin. And after we made love things started rapidly changing. Her sores healed. Her rib cage receded. She had more energy and walked with less of a limp.

When I hear a car pull up, I look out my front window to see Katrina hop out of a taxi and gallop up the steps to my apartment. As I undo the dead bolt on the door, she bursts through slamming into my arms. I stumble backward bracing myself on the back of the couch, reciprocating her forceful hug.

"Well, this is a surprise," I say, with her arms clamped around me, still getting my balance.

"I'm so happy!" She buries her face in my chest.

"What happened? Is everything okay?"

"Of course everything is okay." She looks up at me glowing through tears of joy. "Dave, it went into remission, my cancer. They said it was impossible but it did, I've beaten it for now, we've beaten it!"

I don't know what to say. Holding her in my arms, I start to cry with her. The thing is that I am not sure if mine are tears of joy. My decision not to get treatment, the gun I bought to kill myself, all of my contingency plans down the toilet. It was different before when there was only me. The plan was to fade into the background of life, disconnect myself from everybody, and then pull the trigger. But now I am not going to outlive Katrina. I had never planned for this and now everything needs a serious reevaluation.

"Why aren't you saying anything?" She sniffles.

"Because I am finally happy."

18

The air wafting through the open top of my convertible is hot as I sit, parked for nearly an hour in the smelly back lot of a pawnshop downtown, waiting for it to open. A middle-aged man in an AC/DC t-shirt approaches the two large barred glass doors and unlocks them. It took me a while to conclude that I was going to kill myself. A lot of retrospective thought on life, both my accomplishments and failures. You might say it took my entire life to arrive at the conclusion that I would end it. That is why I am surprised at how quickly I've come to my next decision.

Tired of watching the heat radiate off the asphalt I grab the little black backpack from my passenger's seat and go inside. I am immediately taken aback by all the junk. Floor to ceiling stacks of guitar amplifiers line most of the walls. In front of the amplifiers are racks of guitars. In the center of the room are shelves of CD's and records. On top of those are the DVD racks. Reading an old issue of Hustler magazine, the seedy shopkeeper leans on a glass case full of digital cameras and the accessories to match them. I approach the counter, setting the backpack on top of it.

"Can I help you?" he says, without looking up from his porn.

I point to the bag. "I need to sell this."

Without further instruction he unzips the bag, looks inside and lets out a long whistle.

"That's not legal. I can't sell it," he says, looking back at his magazine. "Barrels sawed too short. Besides, it looks hot."

"Look, it's not stolen. I've got the paper work; it needs a new barrel and stock before it can be used. But it's never been fired. One hundred bucks of work will fetch at least 400," I say, giving my best sales pitch. Irritated, he sighs and looks back into the bag and then up to me.

"What are you expecting to get out of me if I were to ... invest in this?"

My attention is instantly drawn to the jewelry display wedged between the camera accessories and glass pipes. I scan the earrings, necklaces, and gold bracelets, stopping at a glimmering diamond engagement ring.

"Give me that ring and you never see me again. Do whatever you want with the gun."

Without saying a word he heads into the back of the store with the bag. I hear what sounds like a muffled argument between two people and then he returns without the bag. With no sense of urgency he takes out the silver diamond ring and places it into a black felt box, and snaps it closed. He hands me the small box but stops before it reaches my hand, looking me in the eyes for the first time.

"I *never* see you again," he says sternly.

"Agreed," I say, taking the ring.

Sitting in my car for a moment, I take out the tiny black box and flip it open, staring at the ring. I have come a long way, from having no reason to live to wanting to get married. How fast this terrible situation has changed into something wonderful.

I've planned the whole night. I'm going into work early so I can be out by three, giving me enough time to change and pick Kat up at four. We will go to a movie and then over to Le Mousseu's for dinner. The bottle of wine we'll drink will be too much and we will need an after dinner walk through the park to sober up. It sounds corny when I say it in my head. But when we are in front of the stone angel fountain, I will drop to one knee and ask Katrina to marry me. There is no better person to spend the rest of my short life with. And after she says yes and the concrete angel bears witness to our tender kiss, I will tell her that I have scheduled my first chemotherapy session. Clapping the small box shut and tucking it in the side pocket of my cargo shorts, I start the car and drive home.

I awake to someone pounding on my apartment door. It's four in the morning and I have to be to work in two hours. Who the hell could it be this early in the goddamned morning? Groggy, I stumble out of bed, banging my shins on everything in my path. Getting to the door in nothing but my boxer shorts, I open it and am struck by the most horrific sight. It's big fat Sally, with another queer Red Cross t-shirt on, standing in her filthy sweatpants and holding a beat up cardboard box. Her eyes are red from crying and her hands are trembling on the sides of the box.

"Sally?" I say, rubbing the sleep out of my eyes.

"Dave ... I'm so sorry."

"What the hell are you talking about? What's wrong?" I step outside my door to get a closer look at the box she is holding, but it is duct taped shut.

"Katrina died."

"What?"

"They ... they found her ... she ... she committed suicide."

My knees get weak and rubbery, I struggle to stand.

Noise floods my ears. My mind fights to understand. Over the last few months we spent every spare moment of our lives together. She was turning around, getting better ... But really there is no getting better. Gathering every ounce of strength within me I refuse to cry.

"Have arrangements been made?"

"Well, the police say that she had no family ... but she had her affairs in order."

"She knew she was going to do this then?"

"Yes ... here ... it's all here in this letter." Her speech is broken, words strung together by an irritating series of sniffles, sobs, and hiccups. "It was ... it was addressed to you, but the police said they had to open it to declare it a..."

"A suicide, Sally, she committed suicide."

She snaps, going hysterical, wailing and sobbing. She looks at me through tired puffy eyes and thrusts the cardboard box into my chest.

"Take it! It's yours ... she left these things specifically to you."

Sally let's go of the box and runs off, crying. I stand there for a second holding the box in shock. Then I go inside and sit with the box on my lap.

"Oh fuck Kat, what did you do?" I say out loud unsuccessfully trying to wipe away tears that have forced their way from my eyes. But that's not the question I am asking on the inside. On the inside, I ask the question I will hide from everybody, like cancer and like Kat. Another filthy little secret I will forever ask myself: *What did I do to you, Kat?*

I peel the duct tape from the top of the box and open the cardboard flaps. The first thing in the box is a plain envelope with my name handwritten in cursive on it. It's sitting on top of the green and white flannel blanket we used for our rooftop picnic. There are rips along the edge where the envelope was sealed and then torn open. In the distance my cell phone is ringing but I don't care. I stay on the couch with what's left of Katrina. Her whole life condensed into a small cardboard box. Steady streams of warm tears trickle along my jaw line and drip off my chin into the box and on top of the envelope. The ink in my name becomes stained with tears. I remain frozen in time, unable to bring myself to read the letter or look beneath the folded blanket.

The voice mail jingle on my phone goes off, breaking my trance. My phone starts ringing again. I know it's that hypocrite Sally calling to have a dialogue about feelings. That prying bitch read my letter, and now I can't even open it. What does she know about feelings? In that instant, the phone ringing matters, it snaps me awake, inspires a rage inside I haven't felt since I was diagnosed. This is my moment to say good-bye and it's being interrupted. Furious, I set the box on the couch beside me and storm into the bedroom to answer the phone. Maybe chewing somebody out real good will make me feel better. I grab the phone, putting it to my ear without looking at the caller id.

"What?" I scream, losing my temper.

"David?" my mother says in a meek voice.

"Mom? I'm sorry, but can this possibly wait? I'm having a bad fucking day and it's only four in the morning."

"David," she says, and then swallows hard. "David, we need to talk."

I can tell she is crying and can only imagine what the hell else has gone wrong.

"Mom, what's wrong, what happened? Are you and Dad okay?"

"You should come over right now."

"Mom, what's going on?" I try not to shout.

She sniffles and coughs and I hear my dad speaking in the background.

"David, it's your grandmother, she passed away last night."

"I'll be right over." I hang up without saying good-bye.

Numbness washes over my entire body. I never took my own life seriously around Kat, throwing around suicide like a wild card. All the while, learning from group the stress of recovery and witnessing the depths of despair post-recovery depression can bring on. Survivor's guilt. My entire world cracks at the seams. I tear the nicotine patch from my arm. Gram is dead. Kat is dead. Soon, I will be dead.

Which is fine, I feel dead.

It's been eight days since Katrina and Grandma died. I knew my life would change but I never thought life would be this different. The days following their deaths have been hectic and empty. The first was spent in the company of family. Everyone gathered in my grandparent's kitchen supporting my grieving grandfather. People wept and talked about how sudden it was while I passed out numb hugs, pretending to grieve for Grandma. It's not that I wasn't sad, but she was in poor health. Congestive heart failure had filled her lungs with fluid. Diabetes had swollen and distorted her limbs and rendered her kidneys inoperable, while smoking had turned her lungs into thick black paperweights. But she died in her sleep, at home, and that's all that matters. She was happy. Katrina's suicide was a shock. It would have been different if she had died bedridden of cancer. I had imagined it many times. A mental picture of me by her side, holding her hand and ushering her into the afterlife with all the love and affection I have to offer. I never thought she would get better, and then kill herself.

Unable to deal with the situation at hand I retreated behind my grandfather's garage, pacing and chain smoking. My mom came out every so often to get a break from the escalating bickering and sneak cigarettes from me. But we never said a word. I watched as my relatives began to leave, they were carrying things. Some had piles of old books, or random boxes. Plastic bags full of the groceries I had bought. Aunt Deb had a small bust of Michelangelo that sat on an end table beside my grandma's bed for the last 30 years. It's so weird, one of my cousins was even carrying the stack of magazines that had sat beneath the police scanner. Vultures, picking apart the decayed organs that are my grandparent's possessions. Only my grandfather's not dead. In fact I could hear him hammering and wrenching on an old truck through the side wall of the garage. Hammering as my relatives flocked away from this place with everything that would have reminded him of his wife. Hammering as none of them even stopped to say goodbye. Disgusted, I went inside and collapsed on the couch, and spent the night in that lonely house with him.

Now I'm stuck sitting in a stuffy funeral parlor staring at a dull yellow shag rug beneath my feet, surrounded by puke color combinations of browns and greens that stink of the 1970's. From the grimy glass on the framed diplomas hanging beside the window to the dusty finish on the organ by the entrance, nothing shines. This place is constricting. This place is death. My tie is too tight.

Only a few family members have been called before the service for the reading of my grandmother's will. Me, my parents, and my grandparent's three other children and their spouses. It looks more like a small crowd than a family. My aunts and uncles tried to have their kids sit in but the director asked them to leave. My grandpa asked not to be in the room; he is having a hard enough time dealing with her death. Nobody was to be present except for those in the will. My parents and I are already uncomfortable knowing that I am the only grandkid that made it to the will.

Against my grandma's wishes the family had her cremated to lessen the funeral costs. Preoccupied with Katrina's death I wasn't there to fight for her, and when I was around I was a zombie. When I finally realized what was going on, it was too late to do anything about it. The guilt is overwhelming, infuriating. I turn to my dad, so angry that heat is streaming off my face.

"How long do you think this is going to take?" I ask, not caring about the other family members present.

"David, try to have a little—"

"A little what, dad, respect? How about a little respect for the deceased? But I guess you can't un-cremate somebody, can you?"

"What the hell do you know about her wishes?" My aunt condescends.

I turn my head and stare at her, my eyelids narrowed, fists clenched. "Oh, what the fuck ever, Deb. Like you even knew her."

"You watch your tone, boy!" Her husband Nigel stands up in defense, pointing his finger at me. Intimidating Uncle Nigel. He is four times the size of me with tree trunk arms thick with veins and muscles. His skin the hot yellow-orange of whatever cheap spray tan he uses daily. This man looks more like a juiced up gorilla nut job that belongs on a retired beach volleyball team. All of our lives he has pushed us around and bullied us at family events. Not anymore.

"Fuck you, Nigel. You don't scare me," I say, waiving my finger of judgment at everyone except my parents. "And, since today is the last time I will see any of you, there is something I want you all to know. You all make me sick; after your behavior at the house; squabbling over petty bullshit, acting like Grandpa was already dead. You're disgusting, pitiful, selfish."

Nigel balls up his left fist and takes a menacing step towards me as the director returns with the will.

"Well, hello again, everybody." His cheerful disposition disarms our confrontation, for now. Let us be seated. I hope we are all ready for this reading?"

Nigel and I take our seats as directed. The funeral director sits behind his musty looking wooden desk and opens the folder.

"In the last wishes of the deceased there will be no formal reading of the will and testament. You have all been mailed letters indicating your inheritance."

There is a hushed silence followed by a few murmurs of surprise and then finally a reaction.

"What about the money?" My Aunt Deb asks, leaning forward in her seat, clutching the new Coach handbag she sold the bust of Michelangelo to buy.

My grandmother is dead. There will be no more afternoon Scrabble visits. No more evening talks. We will never taste another one of her homemade meatballs on spaghetti night. We will never be woken up by an early morning phone call to hear the latest gossip. And the only thing on her mind, on any of their minds, is money. How much is there? Where is it? When do we get it? Unable to contain my rage, I throw in a comment that is sure to be the catalyst my family needs to implode.

"There is no money," I say.

"How the hell would you know? Of course there is money," Nigel barks.

I recline in my chair, happy the fuse is lit. Nigel slams his fist on the director's desk, his voice booming. Another uncle bellows at him for getting angry. The voices in the room have intensified to blustering shouts, distorted by anger and greed. All the voices in the room erupt except for my parents and mine. I palm a cigarette and lighter out of my suit coat pocket and leave the small office.

Their behavior is embarrassing. No amount of money will fill this emptiness. I take a drag and have a seat on the steps leading out of the small office and let my mind drift briefly to thoughts about Katrina. People arrive in droves for the service which starts in a few minutes. I wonder if the guests hear the muffled screams through the wall. Let them fight it out, it doesn't matter, I don't need anything. She did well by me and doesn't owe me a thing. The oak door to the funeral director's office swings open and smacks into the house. The doorknob whacks the house so hard it cracks the white vinyl siding. What used to be my family bursts out like an angry mob clambering their way around the side of the house. My parents come out last, in tears. I wait on my step; invisible to the monsters. As they pass, I fire off a thought.

"You can all go to hell," I say with a bloodshot teary-eyed smile.

They turn and stare at me and my parents. They look like a pack of rabid animals, raw and visceral. Ready to tear the head off anything that bleeds money. There's a few muttered swears as they turn back around and march into the funeral home. Wiping the tears from my eyes, I put my arms around both of my parent's shoulders.

"Shall we?" I say.

The service was pathetic. I'm so disgusted with my family I can't bear to sit up front. Instead I elect to sit in the back of the funeral parlor with acquaintances that barely knew her. I take a single empty seat between two women I don't recognize. Halfway through the service, the woman to my left tries making conversation. She asks how I knew the deceased. Smiling, I tell her I'm reviewing the funeral home for a local paper. She gives me a queer look but stops talking to me, mission accomplished. The priest from my grandmother's church was unavailable, so a junior priest is leading the service. He looks uncomfortable, like this is his first funeral. Beads of sweat cascade down his face. I can even make out a trace of dark pit-stains when he raises his hand to tug at his collar. He mispronounced both her first and last name and nobody corrected him. Nobody stopped him at all. Nobody stepped up to say kind words about her, nothing. Everyone just stood by as this stranger condensed 77 years into 18 minutes. Nobody even gave a proper eulogy.

A short while after the service I'm walking with my parents across the parking lot of the funeral home when I see Nick approaching us.

"I didn't see you up front," he says.

"Nope," I light a new cigarette with the butt of my old one.

"Hey Mrs. S., my family wants to extend their deepest sympathies." He hugs my mom and then shakes my dad's hand. He walks up to me and gives me a tight hug. "Are you guys going back to your grandparent's for the dinner?"

We look at one another for a minute as if we are considering more degradation. Then my parents look to the ground without a word.

"We're going to do our own thing. It's not like we're welcome anyways."

111

"Well, I go where you go so I'm sticking with you guys. Hey, where's Kat?" Nick says.

His question pierces my heart like a dagger. Not sure what to say, I choose to ignore him for now. I look at my mom and dad sensing the sadness and pain deep inside their hearts and behind their eyes.

"You two should go. Be with the family. Christ, they only hate me."

"David, we want to be with you. We know how close the two of you were and how hard this must be. And we want to do anything we can to help," my mom says.

Anything to help, she says. If she only knew everything. Well, maybe it's time I told her some of the truth. After all, I still have unfinished business.

I turn to my mom, "Could you do me a favor?"

"I've already told you, anything you want."

"Pick me up at my place in an hour and bring Nick." I get into my car quickly, slamming the door.

When Nick and Mom finally get to my house I'm on the front steps, finishing my third beer. I crunch the empty can, chucking it across the front yard and get into the car, stretching my legs out across the backseat. Dad's not with them.

"Where's Dad?"

"Your father went to run damage control with the family, you know how he is."

"Fine."

"Where are we going?" she asks.

"To the city morgue." Both of them perk up in their seats as soon as I say that.

"Excuse me?" Her face scrunches up like a bulldog and she eyes me in the rearview mirror.

"Here," I say, tossing her handwritten directions on a piece of crumpled paper.

Silence from the front of the car. My mom sits with the directions in her hand looking at Nick. This is the most

113

uncomfortable I have ever seen them. He turns in his seat looking at me over the center console.

"I think what your mom meant to say is; why are we going to the morgue?"

"Eight days ago my girlfriend Katrina committed suicide. I have been so wrapped up in Grandma's funeral that I haven't been able to view her body, let alone grieve. We're going to the morgue because I need closure."

My poor mother, face contorted in confusion and tragedy. She had an idea I was seeing somebody, but this must still come as a shock. However she is a good woman and has always supported me. Reluctant, she puts the sedan in drive and pulls out onto the road.

For a couple of miles it is quiet. Not serene, peaceful quiet; it's the type of quiet you would hear center storm before a hurricane splits open a trailer and eats a baby. There is a foul stink of tension and anxiety in the air. I sit, staring out the window like a statue. Never once looking to see if the other two are watching me. The city rots as we wind our way from the suburbs to the inner city. When the street signs begin marking that we are closing in on the morgue, Nick clears his throat. I catch him exchanging glances with my mom, willing each other to speak. Again he turns in his seat to face me.

"Hey man."

"Yeah?" I look deep into his eyes, trying to project the fierce coldness inside me straight to his soul.

"Well, I was wondering—"

"Leave it alone."

"But—"

"I said leave it alone. Do you think I want to talk about this right now? Please, let it be."

He faces front without another word. The car jerks, bouncing over a pothole as my mom turns into the morgue parking lot, slowing to let a pedestrian cross. Maybe it's the idea that death surrounds this place but it looks disgusting from the outside. Old wrappers and broken bottles are strewn about on the sidewalks. The people here all look worn out. They mill about the streets aimless, taking up space. As we are walking around to the front of the building a homeless man in a filthy jean vest and torn brown sweatpants approaches us.

"Hey buddy, can I bum a smoke?" He croaks, extending a dirty fingerless gloved hand in my face.

I look him over before taking out three and handing them to him.

"Hey, thanks kid."

Without a word I continue onward to the entrance. When the glass doors come into view anxiety gets the best of me and I start jogging up the steps.

"You don't have to do this," Nick calls out from behind me. I ignore him.

My mom rushes ahead of me, slamming her hand on the door. I growl at her, hand on the door knob, but check my

115

emotions when I see the worry behind her pink watery eyes. She puts a hand on my shoulder.

"David, before you go into this building, I want you to stop and think about what you're doing. I don't know who she was. This is all … it's all a lot to deal with. For both of us. But I do know that nothing you do in there is going to bring her back."

"Mom I have to, for closure. I have to see her one last time."

She takes her hand off the door and looks away from me. She's crying. After pausing for a second to gather my courage, I pull open the glass doors and head to the receptionist's desk. I tell the young lady why we are there and she pages a medical assistant, who escorts us to the morgue.

This emotionless little twerp in turquoise scrubs opens the tiny cell and slides her out. Her body is draped head to toe in a plain white sheet with greasy stains on it. The morgue technician asks if I'm ready. I hear Nick and my mom both say from behind that I don't need to do this. In the back of my head I know that I shouldn't do this. On my command the technician pulls the sheet down to her chest right above her breasts. The upper slices from the autopsy are visible. I lurch forward, grabbing her stiff lifeless body, trying to give her one last hug. It doesn't feel like Katrina, she's cold and hard like an old piece of wood. Hysterical, I lose strength in my legs; I fall to the floor, taking most of the sheet with me. Clutching my stomach, a soccer-ball sized lump of vomit claws its way up my throat. Violent and hot it forces its way out of my mouth and onto the tile floor. I hear someone yell, "That's enough!" as my vision blurs. The next few moments are populated with distant sensations. The pressure of someone lifting under my arms. The rumbling car engine and its vibrations along my spine. My stomach turning the process of digestion into cramp, expel, repeat. Similar to the instructions on a bottle of shampoo. But these sensations continue to grow distant and dull until the whole world is blotted out.

I wake up in Katrina's bed, drenched in sweat. My silk pajamas caked on my body. Last week is a faded nightmare. Pulling her feather comforter up around my chin and hugging it tight, I feel safe and warm here. I roll over to wake her up but she is already gone, maybe making breakfast or showering. I sit up and dangle my feet off the side of the bed, rubbing yellow sleep crust out of my eyes. Still a little groggy I walk out into the kitchen and then into the living room looking for Katrina.

"Kat?" I call out. "Babe, are you still home?" There is no answer.

I grab my cigarettes off the coffee table and meander out onto the balcony. The breeze chills me in these damp pajamas. I didn't look at the time but it must be early because the entire city around Kat's neighborhood is silent. No cars or buses or screaming kids, nothing. Leaning over the railing, I take a deep drag and enjoy the peace. As I exhale, two arms wrap around my waist from behind.

"Thought you quit?" Kat says in a playful voice.

"You're home." I flick the rest of my cigarette off the balcony and wiggle in her grasp until we're facing. "I thought you left," I say, squeezing her tight.

"And where would I go without you?" She finishes her sentence with a quick peck on the lips.

"Baby, I had the worst dream—"

"Shh." She puts her index finger over my lips. "We have to get going soon; you can tell me all about it after I shower." She gives me one more kiss and then walks inside.

"Maybe I'll join you."

I hear her start the water for the shower and lean my back on the railing. There is a whole world out there waiting for us. I step inside to get ready for wherever we're supposed to go.

"Where are we going today?" I call to Kat from the living room. She doesn't answer. I walk down the hallway repeating the question. She doesn't answer. "Katrina, should I dress nice?"

At the edge of the hallway all I hear is running water and the only thing I see is the bathroom light flickering like a strobe. Concerned, I race to the bathroom door and my feet splash in a puddle of water seeping from underneath. I yell at her to open the door but she doesn't. Panic sets in and fear builds within me. I put my shoulder into the bathroom door and pop it open. To my surprise Katrina is showering.

"Coming to join me?" she giggles.

"Why weren't you answering me? And why is there water all over the floor?" I say.

She pulls open the curtain, water glistening off her naked body. "I didn't hear you. Could you hand me a towel?"

I grab a towel off the hook on the bathroom door and hand it to her as the bathroom lights go out. Pressing my back against the wall I swipe my hand blindly to turn the lights on. Before my hand finds the switch they pop back on and begin flickering. I slip on the wet tile and fall to my knees making a small splash in the inch of water accumulating on the floor. Katrina is floating in the overflowing bathtub, bloated and blue. Floating in the water with her is a wilted rose and a stereo still plugged into the wall. On the toilet is a cardboard box duct taped shut with an envelope lying on top. Quickly I unplug the stereo and crawl to the tub. I turn off the water and put my hands on the porcelain edge.

"Oh my god, Oh my god! Kat, baby, you're going to be okay!"

I reach into the tub, hook my arms around her waist and hoist her out. Her body is stiff and freezing cold. Her small frame weighs a thousand pounds. Sliding on the wet floor I fight to get her out of the tub, but to no avail. I lose my footing and topple into the tub with her, sending water everywhere. After a few more minutes of wet struggle I give up lifting her and lie there. I lift my head above the water and look at her face. Her once white skin is now stained with the bruised color of death. I run the back of my hand along her grainy cheek, my insides becoming a painful pit of despair. I lean in to give her one last kiss. Her eyes snap open wide, glazed with cataracts, devoid of color. She lifts her head out of the water looking straight at me.

"Where's my towel?" she gargles, spitting soapy water into my face.

When I wake up in my room everything is gray and the bedding is soaked with sweat. I look around the room, disoriented, but silently thank God that I'm home. I am wearing pajamas, my suit is wadded up on the floor in front of the closet. My bedroom window is closed which means I wasn't awake when I got here. I sit up, and swing my feet off the side of the bed. My cigarettes aren't on the nightstand, which means my mom probably put me here. Trying to stand, my legs buckle. Collapsing forward I barely catch myself on the wall. My legs are like rubber, my throat burns, and my head is pounding. Like a zombie I shamble out into the living room. When he sees me hobbling in, Nick rushes over and puts his arm around me helping me to a chair.

"Holy shit he's alive."

"Ugh ... of course I'm alive," I say, rubbing my face.

"How are you feeling, kiddo?" My mom comes into the room carrying a tray of soup and sandwiches. "You're up in time for lunch."

"I'm not hungry."

"Well, I made extra in case you woke up so please try to eat."

Sitting at the dining room table and swirling the spoon in my soup I get lost in the alphabet noodles. Watching the individual letters bob and dip in a sea of carrots and green beans. Every swish of my spoon brings about a new combination of letters but never a word. I dip the spoon again and watch, up floats a K, and then an A. Before anymore rise I crush a handful of crackers over the top of it.

"Who was she, David?" my mom says breaking the silence.

Nick freezes in his seat. My brain goes into a rage overload. When she asks about Kat, a switch flips inside my head. My body pumps adrenaline through my rapidly constricting veins. A line of perspiration forms across my brow. My hand begins shaking so bad the spoon is clinking in the ceramic bowl. It forces almost a werewolf like change, turning me into an animal, a beast. I stand up punching my fist into the wall next to the window, smashing a big hole in the drywall and skinning my knuckles bloody.

"Get out of my fucking house!"

"Calm down—"

"Calm down? Calm down? Do I look like I need a fucking interrogation? Get the fuck out of my house right now."

They don't fucking care and how could they? Against their wishes I usher them both outside, ignoring their pleas. Screaming and swearing I slam the door shut and lock the dead bolt. How could they fucking care at all? They don't know anything. Walking back into the dining room and sitting in front of my soup it hits me. They don't know because I haven't told them. I pick up my bowl of soup and hurl it at the wall. In explodes into a bright red Rorschach blotch of broken ceramic chunks. I fall to the floor and cry myself to sleep underneath the dining room table.

It's not that I don't want to see anybody, well actually it is. I haven't made another scene after throwing my mom and Nick out of my house. Instead, I simply try to disappear. To dull this heartache with an injection of loneliness and solitude. I never went back to work because it was easier than saying goodbye. Spend 40 hours a week for a few years with the same people and then suddenly cut them out. I would say it leaves a hole inside, but in my case it only makes the current hole deeper. An emptiness that only serves to strengthen this disease, and weaken me.

I took the spare key out from under my doormat and threw it in the garbage.

A self-imposed exile.

No more people who care left for me to hurt. There are no more lies when there are no more people to ask questions. It seemed so easy in my head. Just walk away.

Earlier in the week, I freaked out and grabbed a stapler covering all of my windows with the darkest blankets I could find. And now, sitting on my leather couch, not sure if it is day or night, I mourn. A single candle burns in the center of my coffee table. The song *Paint It Black* by The Rolling Stones blares from my stereo speakers. I put a cigarette between my lips and light it off of the candle flame. The oxygen from the first puff sends the flame shooting up, singeing my eyebrows.

I don't do much anymore.

On my best days I sit and stare at Katrina's box. I never open it. But I do crack open a can of cheap beer and drink myself to sleep. Drink away the recurring nightmares of Katrina, if only by blacking out.

At my worst I turn off the music and wander from room to room in silence. My footsteps always lead to the same spot. The dresser in my bedroom that held the shotgun. Sometimes I hold the cool brass handle, unable to pull the drawer open. Sometimes I slide it open and peek inside; hoping to get a glimpse of death, but all I end up seeing is hope. Shattered hope, in the shape of a tiny velvet ring box, proof of something worse than death. And then I remember why I am disappearing. Because there is really no difference in waiting to die and killing yourself.

5

I wake up on my couch disoriented from the darkness. I relight the melted candle in the center of my coffee table and let my eyes adjust to the darkness. Then I light a cigarette off the candle. Other than late night runs for beer and cigarettes it's been three weeks since I went outside. Knocks on the front door come and go. My phone is still by the couch plugged into the wall charger, right where my mom left. Like the knocking, the phone rings periodically. I don't respond to either. Sometimes I worry the police will burst through my door expecting to find a corpse swinging from the ceiling fan. But as long as I pay the rent and electric bill, it will be a while before worry pushes people that far. There is at least four months of bill money in my savings account. As long as the rent is paid on time, I can remain in solitude for as long as I want. The thought of finances drifts around my tumor and into my frontal lobe. The rent. Snatching my wallet off the recliner, I run out the door and immediately shield my eyes from the blinding blast of midday sunlight. Retreating inside I grab my sunglasses and then dash down the block.

"Can I help you, sir?" The female bank teller smiles at me despite my appalling appearance and stench.

The random thought of bills has reminded me the rent hasn't been paid this month. An eviction notice could fuck up my disappearing act. But in a hasty departure I hadn't changed my clothes. I'm still wearing the same blue bathrobe, pajama bottoms and t-shirt that I woke up in after seeing Katrina in the morgue. The sudden cleanness of the outside world reveals how ripe my stench is. A walking mass of foot and crotch odor mixed with stale beer, and old sweat. I approach the sweet smelling young woman behind the counter in shame, awaiting her judgment.

"I need a money order."

She studies my filth intensely before requesting my driver's license. She shuffles some papers and clicks the computer mouse on her screen a half dozen times. That's when something changes. A subtle shift in body language. Her smile is less forced. It's as if all the sudden, I don't look like a raving lunatic.

"How much sir?"

"Eight hundred and fifty, and can I get a balance inquiry as well?"

She finishes processing the transaction and slides my money order and drivers license across the counter to me. A moment later she hands me the receipt. The figure on the receipt stops me; there are way too many zeroes after the account balance.

"Excuse me; I think there's a problem." I show her the slip, pointing to the massive balance. "Where did all this money come from?"

She looks at her computer screen as lines of numbers scroll in the reflection of her glasses. "No sir, no mistake, these funds transferred into your account over a week and a half ago."

"Thanks." I say, backing away from her towards the exit staring at the balance on my receipt.

A half hour later I'm stinking up the line in the post office with an orange slip that was taped to my P.O. Box. I look like a crazy person. After a week of non-delivery they started withholding my mail. I walk up to the postal clerk and present my slip. It takes him a little while to bring back the massive white plastic bin from their storage room. I never thought that three weeks of mail would look so mountainous. After being chastised for letting my mail build up I buy a stamp and slide the rent check into the outgoing mail slot.

At home I dump the mail onto my couch frantically spreading it about and searching until I see it. An ominous brown envelope with the lawyer's insignia in the upper right corner. It's my inheritance. Fuck. I tear it open, slide the paperwork out and sit on my mail littered couch. I rifle through its contents until I find the right pages, discarding the rest on the floor. It says exactly what I thought it would. My inheritance transferred three and a half weeks ago. And it's sizable. Enough for me to live quite comfortably until I die. Suddenly I'm rich and, in a way, this is the supreme kick in the head. God's little punch line before he sends me packing on the brain tumor train to hell. Somebody has some explaining to do.

It took over an hour in the shower to clean myself. It felt great but still didn't refresh me, I'm exhausted. The sun is setting when I pull into my grandfather's driveway. The massive house is dark. Nobody answers the front door. Knowing it won't be locked I open it and call out to my grandfather, no answer. The big wooden door lets out a slight creak and echoes in the empty house when I close it. The smell of Pine-Sol hits me. I flick on the kitchen lights and choke back tears. Everything is gone. The kitchen table and chairs, the dishes, the pantry and cupboards are bare. No screeching Morse Code tones and no buzzing hum of an oxygen machine. The smell of coffee and cigarettes are gone, replaced by plug-in air fresheners and new paint. Disturbed, I back right out of the front door. This isn't the house I grew up in anymore. Walking back to my car I see a flicker of light coming from the garage. Then the loud hum of an air compressor kicks on. I go inside to find my grandpa cutting apart the chassis of a large truck with a blowtorch. He stops and flips his helmet up.

"David, how you doing? Missed seeing you around here the past few weeks."

"Yeah, I'm doing okay, Grandpa. Sorry, I have been real busy with work and all."

"That's good. You work hard and you will do well no matter what you do. As long as you work hard. You gotta keep busy." He fiddles with various mechanic's tools as he talks to me. Picking up screwdrivers and wrenches, only to replace them a minute later. There is nervousness behind his voice. He drops his welder's helmet to the floor and it clangs against a pile of wrenches.

"Are you okay, Grandpa?"

"Yeah I'm fine. Haven't seen many people since Ma passed. I let them take what they wanted and then I guess they all moved on." He picks up a claw hammer and starts pounding on a chunk of metal locked in a vise on his workbench. "You like what I did with the place?"

"It's clean."

"Well, I figure everyone else moved on so no sense staying in a big old house by myself."

"You're selling the house?"

He lets out a long sigh and begins hammering the chunk of metal harder.

"Yeah." He tosses the hammer onto the bench and kneels on a greasy blanket next to his tools, burying his face in his hands. We stay in silence together for a few minutes.

131

Neither one of us sure where this conversation is going. Or where we're going for that matter. Two souls, lost without our mates.

I kneel on the blanket next to him and put my hand on his shoulder. "You know why I'm here don't you."

"Yes. The money." He makes the word money sound like a swear word.

"Why? That must be like your entire retirement. You two didn't need to do this."

"No, it was a fund we had set up. We wanted you to go to college, but when you decided not to, we just kept saving. Figured it couldn't do you harm. This way we knew you'd always be alright."

"But what about the rest of the family?"

"They got what they wanted. Took what they could. We knew it would happen," he says. "They even took her ashes. For the first time in 58 years I'm without your grandmother. They don't deserve anything more."

I study every crease in his worn face and look deep into his tired eyes. "You're not dead Grandpa. You can use this money; I want you to have it."

"I can't do that son. Besides, how long do you think I will make it without her? You need to go out and make us proud, this is your time, your chance. Don't waste it. And start by doing something nice for yourself. You work hard and you deserve it."

Something nice for myself?   He's right, that is something I can do. But first I have to do something nice for him.

"You have to move in there!"

My mom glances across the granite kitchen table to my father and he looks away from both of us. I've been ranting at them, pacing their black and white checkered kitchen floor like it's a padded cell, for at least an hour. Neither one of them can look at me right now. Their denial is too much to deal with. I slam my fist against the table and continue my rant.

"They left him with nothing. You guys have to do something. How could you let him stay over there all alone since the funeral?"

"You need to calm down," she says.

"Calm down? There is an old man dying of loneliness over in that house and you two don't care?"

"Your grandfather is going to be fine." She closes her eyes tight, as if she is trying to imagine me away. To sweep me under this family's dirty little rug to be forgotten. My dad stays silent, taking my mother by the hand.

"Fine? That's how you sleep? You just tell yourself that everything is going to sort itself out."

This is why they don't know I have cancer. This is why I could never have told them about Kat, or group. They would have just closed their eyes and told me that everything is going to be alright. Right up until the moment I went into my coffin, kicking and screaming. They would have stayed silent as it traveled along the conveyor into the oven against my wishes, turning me into a pile of ash they could display when company comes over. Their son, just another possession, the ultimate possession. And for a moment, my mom looks like my aunt. She looks like Sally, like every controlling bitch I've ever met.

"You know what? Fuck you, you have no idea what I've been through."

My mom stands up, pulling her hand from my father's, and takes a step towards me. Confrontation was never her thing but I can tell that she is ready to unleash her maternal fury.

"What you've been through, who do you think you are? You throw me and your best friend out of your house and then disappear. You don't answer your door; you never answer your phone. We thought you were dead," she says. "And then you have the audacity to waltz into our home and yell at us about the state of our family? You think we haven't seen what's happened to your grandfather? No, we have been out here dealing with this mess while you hide crying about your little girlfriend. Get out of my house!"

I stand up so fast I knock the chair over behind me. I pick up a stack of magazines from the table and launch them into the living room. Completely surprised by her reaction, it's all I can do. Her angry face is flushed with red blotches. My stomach is in knots. Dad won't even look at me. They're right. What right do I have to come in here and tell them what to do? The only thing I know is that I am dying and can't move in with him. It wouldn't be right. But then again what is right anymore? And how did everything get so fucked up? Quietly I pick my coat up off the stairs and leave. There's nothing left for me here. They will regret this decision for the rest of their life.

The bar at Le Mousseu is a white leather paradise in the heart of the business district. The only barstool in the city that requires a reservation. Do something nice for yourself. That's what he said. And now I'm wearing my best suit, might have paid a hundred dollars for it at Goodwill two years ago. This isn't really my kind of place; I'd prefer a dive bar thick with cigarette smoke. The kind where the felt on the pool table has questionable stains and the bartender does shots with you. But this place reminds me of Kat, she loved it here. I motion for the bartender and before I lower my hand he is refilling my tumbler with whiskey.

"Excuse me," I say, before he walks away. "Could I buy that bottle right there?" I point to a bottle of Chivas Regal Royal Salute. *Aged fifty years* is etched into the gold plate stamped onto the front of the bottle. The bartender chokes when I request it. He adjusts his maroon bow tie.

"Sir," he pauses and leans in closer to me, "are you aware of the price on—"

"Stop," I cut him off. "I gave you my credit card." I drain my glass of whiskey in one swig and slide the empty tumbler towards him. "My bottle please." He produces a small key on a silver chain from the breast pocket of his suit coat and retrieves my liquor.

Rich, alone, drunk, and unhappy. This is how I find myself six months after being diagnosed terminally ill. I hear the porter escort someone to the plush white leather bar seat next to me. The scent of Elegance by Johan fills the air in my space, choking me up a bit. Elegance was Katrina's favorite perfume. I remember the tiny pink glass bottle she kept on the stand by her apartment door. The last thing she would do before we left was lightly mist herself with it. I don't want to look, I shouldn't look, but I do.

Sitting next to me, ordering a dirty martini, is a gorgeous brunette. Her dress flows like a river of black satin, subtly accentuating her curves, drawing my attention upward to her hazel eyes. Around her neck is a diamond chandelier necklace. It looks like the 18k white gold Lucello my dad got for my mom on their 20th wedding anniversary. I remember seeing the ticket price and wondering if he had spent the entire 20 years saving for it. She is so far out of my league I start to sweat just looking at her. I look straight ahead searching for something else to concentrate on. I fixate on a bottle of Black Velvet behind the bar and read the label over and over. My eyes drift upwards and I notice her eyeing me in the mirror. I finish my glass of Chivas and pour another trying to ignore her. Concentrating all of my negative energy on getting her to leave, choose another seat, go somewhere else. She shifts in her seat and I can feel her eyes searing the side of my face. I know what happens next. She says excuse me. Reluctant, I turn slightly and look at her.

"Forgive me for sounding cliché, but what is a guy like you doing in a place like this?"

"Who exactly is a guy like me?"

"Well, you're good looking, and you're alone in the nicest restaurant in this city, drinking a bottle of the most expensive liquor they have to offer."

"You flatter me."

"I'm not done, your suit is cheap. It's nice, but it's cheap. And you're wearing sneakers? Your appearance doesn't add up."

"Sorry, thought it was obvious what I was doing."

"And that is?"

"Drinking." I take another sip.

"Well, that is obvious, but what brings you here? Are you on the run? Stolen someone's identity and going on one last hurrah? Drinking to celebrate? Drinking to mourn?"

"Drinking to forget."

"I can drink to that." She toasts me and we clink glasses.

"What do you do?" she asks after taking a sip.

"Self-employed."

"Ah, me too." She finishes her martini and I flag the bartender and order another for her. Maybe this is the human contact I need right now. "It gets lonely though, missing out on the human contact of having a nine to five."

An hour and a half later we are drunk. Not the get to know you drunk either. We are the slobbery, filthy, laying all over each other drunk. She is sitting on my lap when I realize that we are going to fuck before the night is out. Even with my senses impaired it's hard to imagine taking anyone else to bed other than Katrina. Her ghost haunts my every advance on this woman. This beautiful woman with her hard, perfect body. When the time comes will I be able to fuck this stranger? I hear my grandfather's voice in the back of my head, *Do something nice for yourself.* She slides her free hand around the back of my neck and pulls me close. The pungent odor of martini olives on her breath.

"Let's get out of here," she whispers while nibbling my ear. I throw my hand up flagging the bartender.

"Close us out."

I'm fumbling, trying to get my shoes and pants off as she pulls the long black dress over the top of her head. No bra, no underwear, just her high heels and jewelry. I place my half empty bottle of Chivas on the nightstand. Hurried and horny we don't pull back the sheets or blankets; we fall backwards onto the bed collapsing into each other. She sits on top of me and gives me a devious grin. I smile back, marveling at the design of this beautiful specimen. For the first time I notice the highlights of blonde streaked throughout her brown hair. But, underneath her on this hotel bed, my hands around her supple body, I feel nothing but empty, if it's possible to feel a void. My hand caresses her silky waist and I miss the ridges of my corpse bride's ribcage. When she leans over, her hair falls onto my face. Her ass is firm, not bony. I pause from foreplay for a second and realize that she will never be Katrina. Nobody will ever be Katrina.

"I need a condom."

Her arm wisps down the side of the bed and into a red pocketbook. She sits back up on top of me and fans out three different colored packages.

"A working girl always comes prepared," she says with a smile.

I grab the blue one and think about Katrina. I think about every unique curve of her frail body. I think of the way she felt in my arms afterwards. And now the emptiness she left behind in a wake of self-destruction. Then I close my eyes and fuck this complete stranger.

I awake an hour later to the rustling sound of clothes being jostled about. Rolling onto my side I look around the dimly lit room. The woman stands by the door with her satin dress and high heels on. She is sending a text message on her phone. I watch her for a few minutes before she realizes I woke up.

"Hey stud, how are you feeling?"

"Tired," I say, rolling onto my back.

"Well, I have to get going so we have to make good."

Closing my eyes my brain starts to arrange the puzzle pieces I missed throughout the night. The questions at the bar, the expensive clothing, the condoms, what girl carries condoms? A working girl. My heart begins to race as I decide how to handle this. But unfortunately I short circuit.

"Um … huh?" Is all I manage to say.

She stares at me for a second before her face contorts in bewilderment.

"Um … money?" She produces a small laminated card from her pocketbook. "Here, a list of rates for all the services I provide."

I sit up on the edge of the bed and snatch the small card out of her hand. She is fucking serious. I should have known. It's too late to do anything but pay her and yet my brain doesn't know how to process this situation. The card in my hand is like a buffet menu that I've already pigged out on.

"You're a whore?"

As soon as the word whore leaves my mouth her slap connects with my face. "I am a call girl, there's a difference."

Scanning the price list she is right about that. Again I try and approach this with finesse but my mouth still doesn't want to cooperate.

"Is this a fucking joke? I'm not paying you this."

She leans in close examining the card.

"Yes you are. And by my count that will be eleven hundred dollars." She reads a text message and then responds. "I do understand how this might be confusing so I'm going to clear things up for you."

She opens the door to the room and in walks one of the biggest men I have ever seen. He calmly walks over to me and with no strain at all lifts me by my neck, thrusting me into the wall. He is holding me so high I see a thick purple scar on the top of his massive shaved head. Suspended in mid-air, my windpipe crushed, I claw at his hands.

"Go easy on him, Larry, I like this guy."

"You gonna pay now?" his deep voice bellows out.

Unable to speak from my throat being simultaneously crushed and strangled, I do nothing more than dangle for a bit. He balls up his other fist, massive and solid like concrete, and then slams it into my stomach and drops me to the floor. After gasping for air I look up at them.

"My wallet, please," my voice squeaks and rasps.

She withdraws my wallet and a single cigarette from the nightstand. She places the cigarette between my lips and lights it.

"You look like you need one, love," she says, handing me my wallet.

I take out fourteen hundred dollars and hand it over to her. The most cash I've ever had on me at once gone in a single night of debauchery.

"Thanks for the tip, love." She smiles and hands me a business card. "Although your etiquette lacks finesse, keep my card in case you ever get the urge." She and Larry leave and it's quiet.

I crawl across the floor reaching up to the television stand for the bottle of Chivas and take a big swig, and then another.

My brain pulses against my skull like it is swelling and cracking in half. The stink of my apartment is making me sick and so is being alone. I roll off the couch onto the floor and pick up the closest dirty t-shirt. Stretching it over my head I get a big whiff of feet and dried whiskey. This is my life. Dragging ass to the door I get ready for a much needed walk. Being this low, a little sunshine and fresh air can't hurt. I close my eyes and throw open the front door preparing for my reemergence into the brightness of the outside world. My eyes open slow, giving them time to adjust to the morning sun, but it's dark. Everything is pitch-black except for the distant yellow glow of the streetlights. Fishing around in my pocket for a minute I retrieve my cell phone. Eighteen missed calls and 27 new voicemails, but I don't care. It's 11 at night, I don't remember how long I was asleep or when the last time I went to bed was. I go out the door anyways. My luck is on the downside lately so who cares if I slept through one day, or five or six of them. Lighting up a cigarette I thrust my hands in my pockets and wind through the sidewalks of the city. The world looks different now, gray and ugly. It's like someone reached into my brain and stripped out all the color. I pass by my favorite bar. It is jam-packed, people spill out the door as a local punk band shakes the bordering buildings. I don't go in. I haven't had the urge to go to a bar since the incident with the hooker.

"Hey man, got a dollar?" A scrubby looking homeless guy breaks my thought.

I keep walking without any acknowledgment. I can hear him tell me to fuck off as I walk away. I'm not a part of this world anymore, only an invisible observer. I am terminally ill, but I already feel dead. Like a ghost traveling along roads of the past.

A warm breeze tickles the whiskers of my two-week old beard. This city is like a polluted lake. The storefront windows reflect my horrific and distorted reflection. I wind my way through seedier parts of town. I pass through an abandoned industrial complex and then into a neighborhood where the houses are mostly empty. Plywood with jagged nails sticking out cover smashed and missing windows. Every once in a while I pass a telephone pole decorated with stuffed animals and pictures in memorial for someone who was shot and killed. As I walk through the carnage of urban decay my head starts to throb. This is a more familiar pain, not my sickness, this is a hangover. The sleepy-sick achy headache has grown more frequent in the past month. A definite sign of my steady travel along the path of alcoholism. Since Katrina died it's like I'm navigating a ship through sea of booze. I stop and rest on a graffiti covered bench next to a smashed up bus stop. The bus sign is missing; it looks as if somebody drove their car through it. Sitting here at this bus stop, all my avenues feel exhausted. I place my head in my hands and wonder where people with nowhere left to turn go.

Then I remember. When I was a kid, my grandmother dragged me to church until I was 10. And when I say dragged I mean by my ear. We were the only two in my family who attended. Every Sunday, it was terrible. But she would always tell me that no matter what happens He will always be there for me. I have never been one to turn to God, but desperate times call for desperate measures.

I rise from the squalor of my bench and make my way through the city to a slightly more civilized part of town. As the cracks in the sidewalk decrease my mood turns. There is a new vigor growing inside me as I approach the massive cathedral. The church before me is nothing like the one I remember from my youth. Or the one that hosted meetings where I met Kat. This Catholic monstrosity is a monument to God with its towering peaks and looming stained glass windows. Nervous, I look at my cell again; it's getting late, but never mind that, priests have to listen. Charging up the concrete steps I throw my body into the door excited about the prospect of telling someone the truth, about my disease, about Katrina's suicide, about everything.

147

My body is met by the deadening blow of a giant wooden door that doesn't budge an inch. Dazed, I stagger backwards barely able to keep from falling off the concrete steps. Closed? Is church allowed to be closed? The door handle is locked. Surely there have been people in the past seeking salvation in the middle of the night. Furious I bang my fists into the wooden doors. Pounding, punching, kicking, hammering, and slamming the doors with all my might. I pound until the wood splinters against my bloody, swollen knuckles. Crying I pound until I hear a latch click on the other side.

"You can't sleep here," an old voice says as the door creaks open. "There is an open mission on Basalt Ave. I can't help you."

When the door opens an old man in a worn red robe and fluffy pink slippers steps into view. The only hint that he might be a man of God is the crucifix hanging from his neck over the top of his filthy undershirt. I sniffle and wipe the tears from my face.

"Are you a priest?"

"Why, yes, my son. And as you can tell I am a tired priest, the good Lord himself took a day of rest, I deserve at least a few hours," he begins tapping his foot.

"Um …"

"Um is not an answer at twelve in the morning. Now unless someone was murdered, we're closed," he snarls and begins closing the door.

"I need someone to talk to," I say, suppressing tears.

"Well, I would be glad to lend you my ear. Come back at seven and we can talk all day long if you like. But until then I'm tired and we're closed!"

He slams the door in my face. Closed, church closed. If I die tonight I will go to hell because I am going to have to remain un-absolved until morning. Rejected. Rejected by my family, by my friends, by Katrina, and now by God. I sit on the concrete steps outside the church and smoke a cigarette. Everything is closed. Shit, the only thing open for a guy like me right now is hell. Maybe my place is among the damned. Then I see exactly what I need right now. Like an oasis in the desert, the unlit neon sign for Cobb's liquor store beckons to quench my thirst for self-destruction. I pick up a red brick from the edging that borders the church's flower garden and head towards the storefront. Crossing the street and closing in on my prey, I see it, unprotected, no iron bars across the huge glass window. Without any hesitation or forethought I hurl the brick through the window. Glass explodes as the brick sails onward finding its home in a Jack Daniels display. Frozen in the middle of the street, terror washes over me. What if there is an alarm system? The cops will be on their way in seconds and take me to jail. The owner will be alerted and he will

149

come, too. There will be fines and jail time and my parent's shame. I shut my brain off for a moment and listen to the quiet night. There is no sound, no alarm in the store, no cars, and no police sirens.

Shards of glass crunch and crackle beneath my sneakers as I step through the broken window. The smell of Jack Daniels permeates the air. I stop for a moment to take in the experience. Every ounce of common sense and reason tells me to run. Fear overcomes me. Still, I advance deeper into the store, fighting my natural flight response and perusing the wine and liquor selection like a connoisseur. I pass through the local wines and then the chardonnays, barely batting an eye. Wine gives me a headache. I need something that cures headaches. Stopping for a brief moment in the scotch section, I browse but decide against stealing any, it's too expensive. Past the scotch section and right before the coolers of boxed wine, I see what I came for. It shines golden in the dark. I had to do a double take because I thought there was a halo over it. Wild Turkey. A half gallon of Wild Turkey. More than enough to kill even the toughest drinker.

"Well, you will do fine, friend," I say to the bottle.

I sit on the curb outside Cobb's and take the cap off my new friend, tossing it into the street. I hold the bottle high above my head, making a toast to nobody.

"Exorcising my demons one sip at a time."

I look to the right up the street and then to the left down the street. To my surprise there are no cops, no bums, no passing cars, and more importantly, no people. Nobody can place me at the crime scene accept a worthless priest who didn't care to ask my name. A few more sips of whiskey and I cross the street into an ally and start to zigzag my way across the city.

After my burglary I decide to keep a low profile for the rest of the night. The last thing I need is to get arrested for drunk and disorderly conduct with a stolen bottle of Wild Turkey. Making my way out of the hood and into the more familiar suburbanized parts of the city, I find myself outside West Havenhurst Cemetery.

Quietly, I stare at all the dead and continue drinking. In elegant cursive, the engraving on the iron sign reads *Gone but not forgotten.* That's such bullshit. I slide my whiskey bottle through two of the iron bars, placing it on the grass, careful not to knock it over. I grab the top of the fence and pull myself up. When I crest the top my grip slips a little and sends me tumbling over the other side. One of the ornamental spikes on the top posts catches my back pocket and slices through my jeans and underwear. I crash to the ground hard, a few feet from my whiskey bottle, the pain stunning me. With the labored, uncoordinated movement of a drunk I roll onto my stomach and touch my ass where the big hole is. No blood. I crawl to the bottle and pick up my binge right where I left off.

My motor functions have gone to shit and it's getting hard to see. I support myself on the gravestones and stumble out of the cemetery where the fence ends by a park. At the edge of the park is a green steel deck bridge that goes over the canal. I have spent many drunken nights under this bridge with Nick reflecting on life. The bridge in the distance is a symbol of the past I left behind. Fitting that I should die beneath it.

I lean against the graffiti-filled cement wall of the bridge, my legs stretched out in front of me. I pick up a small rock and try to skip it into the canal but my hand doesn't receive the signal from my brain. The rock smashes into my foot and skids to a stop in the dirt pathway just short of the water. I hold the bottle up, it's three quarters of the way gone. I'm so close to you, Katrina. I get the spins and black out a few times, images of Nick, Katrina, my grandma, and my family flash in my head. Memories like faded Polaroid's. I miss them. Hell, at this point, I miss anyone that would have listened or loved. I threw it all away.

I hear footsteps echoing in the distance, gravel scraping under each step. Anybody out at this hour is up to no good. I try to stand up but my body doesn't cooperate. It seems the only limb I have any control over is the arm attached to the bottle. I take another swig. It's probably the cops catching up to me, coming to arrest me for drunk and disorderly or breaking and entering. I take another swig. Or it's that homeless guy I slighted earlier coming to knife me in the dark.

I take another swig. Oh well, whatever the comeuppance, it's long overdue. I lean my head against the cool concrete and close my eyes, I am starting to wear out, and it will be over soon.

"Something told me you might be here. What the fuck happened to you?" the stranger says, kneeling next to me.

I look up from my seat halfway to hell. It's Nick. He snatches the bottle out of my hand and takes a drink. A single drop rolls out onto his tongue. I don't speak because I know I can't. He holds the bottle in front of us.

"Wow, you drank all of this?" He throws the bottle into the canal. "Well, time to get you home before you die."

He lifts me up, putting one of my arms around his shoulder to support my deadweight. I struggle against him, falling to the ground and skinning the bottoms of my hands. Lurching forward towards the water, I hurl into the canal.

I awaken on the couch in my dark apartment, a pile of blankets on top of me. My sticky body is glued to the leather with sweat. Lights from the kitchen burn holes through my retinas. On my coffee table are the melted remnants of burned out candles. I feel sick. I roll over and push all the blankets onto the floor. My brain is sloshing against the inside of my skull and my body is in the achy stage right before a raging hangover. Nick walks out of the kitchen carrying two cups of black coffee.

"Jesus Christ, I thought for sure I was going to have to call an ambulance." He hands me one of the mugs. "You're a real fucking soldier you know that?"

I slap the mug out of his hand onto the floor. "Get out."

"Well that's gratitude for you. Asshole, I saved your life."

Saved my life? He only gave me another stay of execution. If I don't destroy myself cancer will. What the hell does he know about saving lives?

"Get out!"

"Look, the people who love you are getting real sick of this pathetic pity party you have been living. Not answering your door, your phone. Quitting your job. Wake the fuck up man. Look around you, this place is disgusting. You're disgusting. You're a drunk; you have to snap out of this, get help if you need to."

I tried not to make a scene after throwing him and my mom out. I wanted to disappear. But it's clear now that you can't always get what you want. I stand up and step forward to confront my now former best friend. This will be for the best, even if I am still drunk.

"I hate you ... and everybody else too ... I want to be left alone ... Why doesn't anybody understand?" I shout. "Everyone grieves different ... and some of us are real fucking content to sit alone in our apartment listening to *Paint It Black* on repeat in the dark! So please leave. I have much pity left to wallow in, asshole."

After my rant Nick stares at me in utter disgust and then throws his cup of coffee on the floor. Turning his back to me he stomps outside. He stops once more before closing the front door.

"You're pathetic."

"Go!" I storm over and slam the door in his face.

Leaning against the door, I let my tears free fall to the carpet. I have alienated everyone so I can die alone. With my face still pressed against the door there are three powerful knocks. The gloom turns to rage and I throw open the door ready to scream. But when the door opens a flash of light sends me sailing backwards inside my apartment. My heel catches on a stray sneaker and sends me ass over head. A whirlwind of old mail and beer bottles flutter about in the chaos as I crash through the living room coffee table. I lie on the ground in disbelief, broken glass and wood and melted hunks of candles jammed into various vertebrae. A shard of glass slices through my t-shirt and warm blood from the wound runs down my ribs.

"You hit me," I say, holding my bloody, crooked nose.

"You left me no choice," Nick says, shaking off the pain of his hand.

"You *hit* me."

"Yeah, I know." He walks into my apartment, covering his nose from the smell. Despite my protests starts yanking the blankets off the windows. Morning sun beams burst into my home assaulting and shocking my eyes. My apartment is in complete disrepair. Dirty clothes and dishes and old food cover the floor. Most of the furniture has been overturned. The refrigerator door is wide open, which explains the smell of rotting, spoiled food. Nick comes and squats next to me.

"Look around man, are you ready to listen to reason?"

I pause for a moment, reassessing the state of my apartment. Is this filth what my life has become? If I died here this would have been my contribution to the world. And this is how I would have been remembered. They would have said things like, *did you hear the way they found him?*

"Okay," I say, giving in.

"Good, I only have one rule for helping you though," he says.

"What?"

"No questions."

"Fine, deal. What's next—"

"Ah! I said no questions."

"Sorry."

"Go get some shoes on while I try to find you clothes. We're going to your parent's so you can shower. And no, I don't want you showering here. I don't trust anything to be clean within these walls."

"No way. My mom hates me."

"Your mom doesn't hate you. You've got the past few months' events skewed inside that fucked up little head of yours. Now come on let's go." He helps me up off the floor.

Outside the warm sun hits my face. It is rejuvenating. Halfway to the car Nick reaches into a plastic bag he is carrying and tosses me a bag of frozen peas.

"At least you left your freezer door closed."

I press the bag under my puffy eye and across my nose and lean my seat back to get more comfortable. We sit in silence in Nick's car. He puts the key in but doesn't start it, staying still, staring at the windshield. He turns to face me.

"We have to talk about Katrina."

My heart begins bashing against my chest cavity. "Sure."

"I'm not trying to be an asshole but I think you got too attached too fast. I mean, how long did you know her? Where did you two meet? I was thinking about it the other day and I don't know anything about her."

It becomes almost impossible to hold back the rotten puke churning in my stomach. I can't tell my best friend anything about the woman I love. How would I explain that we met in a cancer support group? He can never find out that she killed herself because she didn't want to sit around and watch me die. Every single piece of information will only lead him more questions. And all of these roads lead to my inoperable brain tumor. And I'm not ready for him to know about that. How could I tell him about something I can't accept myself? It is time to swallow my pride and bury the truth in more lies.

"You're right. We didn't know each other that long. We met in a coffee shop."

"See, you hate coffee shops, it never would have worked out."

I force out a laugh. "I know... I guess it was the shock that they both died in the same 48 hours."

"That's fair."

"You know you're right. I jumped in way too fast and got too attached. I should have gotten to know her better. Then maybe I would have seen the signs, but at least she didn't take me out with her. I mean, the crazy bitch could have killed me too."

"It's good to hear you coming back to reality." Nick starts the car and drives out onto the street towards my moms.

Katrina, if you can hear me, I didn't mean any of that.

It took almost a week of hauling garbage to fully clean out and sanitize my apartment. At one point I counted 12 black plastic bags of trash at the curb. It's stunning that one person could produce so much waste. And now it's over. We repainted, shampooed rugs, and bleached the tile showers and sink basins white again. It's like someone hit a reset button and I had never lived here. My mom threw out all the ashtrays. They helped me box up a lot of things I don't need anymore. They helped me clear out clutter from the past to make room for the future.

We packed away old ceramic figurines and porcelain dragons my grandma had bought for me. We packed away hundreds of books. Books that spanned from my childhood right up until a few months ago. Nothing phased me, nothing until the atlas at the bottom of my bookshelf. I had turned it on its side and laid it across the other books because it was too big for the shelf. When I saw it I choked. It immediately transported me back to the kitchen table. When I was a boy, my grandmother would flip pages in the atlas. We would eat cheese and crackers as she told me of all the exotic places she had been and all of the places I would go.

She had never been to any of these places. Safaris on the plains of Africa. Walkabouts in the Australian outback. She had never been to the Washington Monument. Hell, she had never been out of the state. But I had a chance. I was the young boy who had all the opportunities that she didn't. Seeing that atlas, it made me want to leave, right then and there. It made me want to steal her ashes, and drive them all over the country, and show her all of the places she never saw. But I couldn't leave.

So now I sit, alone on my couch, in my clutter free white-walled living room. Might as well be a padded cell, scented with bleach and Febreeze. Nick and my parents went home. I have nothing, no job, barely any friends or family. Maybe I could leave. I pick up my cell and dial Nick.

"What's up dude? How ya feeling?" he asks.

"I have to get the hell out of here."

It didn't take him more than 10 minutes to get to my place. For once I can't read him, worry, disgust, anger, nothing. The vibe he is putting off right now is emotional static, white noise.

"Well?" I say, expecting my next chastising.

He paces the length of my living room, right through the spot where my coffee table used to be. "Are you serious?" he asks, calm and cool.

"Yeah, I have to get away."

"And you expect me to just up and leave with you?" He is in front of me now, arms crossed, eyes narrow.

"No it's not that I want—"

"Stop," he waves his hand in the air to silence me. "You've been going through a lot lately, and you've put me through a ton of shit. And it's okay, but now you expect me to just pick up and leave with you? Leave my life? Leave my job?"

"Um …"

"You know, after that stunt you pulled with the drinking and depression, I didn't think you could get any more selfish. Clearly, I was wrong." He approaches me on the couch and places a hand on my shoulder. "You're on your own with this one."

"Nick, dude, stop—"

My cries are futile. Each plea met only with the back of his shirt as he walks away. And then, without a slam, he closes the door behind him. He's right, I am on my own.

THREE

My alarm clock goes off for the last time. I lay awake in my bed for a little while. The walls of my bedroom are bare. Every last bit of my life has been packed into boxes and put into a storage locker. Every box a cardboard coffin for the dead possessions that once defined me. Sitting on the edge of my bed, I rub my face and light a cigarette. In the darkest hours of the early morning I make my way to the living room. I stand in the doorway. Moonbeams shine through the bay windows, adding an eerie glow over the vast, empty room. In the center, on the floor, is a duffel bag with everything I will need for my departure. Folded beside the bag are the clothes that I will wear today. Next to them is Katrina's box.

I drag the oversized olive green duffel bag out my front door to the back of my car. I have already gotten out of my lease and found a new tenant. With nobody left to say goodbye to, I heave the big bag into my trunk and get behind the wheel. I turn the key in the ignition and shift into reverse. As I pull out of my spot, a black SUV comes up behind me, blocking my escape. Nick gets out of the driver's seat and walks up to my window. He looks at me over his red tinted sunglasses. I roll my window down and wait for him to say something.

"You're really serious about this shit?"

"Bet your ass I am."

"Fuck man, you're putting me in a hell of a spot here."

I stare at him from the driver's seat. He leans against my car door, waiting for me to say something, anything. I look at my best friend's face for a long time in silence.

"Listen, Nick, it was good seeing you before I leave, but I have to go."

"Fine, I understand, just let me move my truck."

"Thanks."

Nick walks back to his truck and, to my surprise, opens the cab, takes out a small duffel bag and two suitcases, and then walks to my car. He opens the door and starts cramming his stuff in.

"What the hell are you doing?"

"You're not going anywhere without me. So I am going to finish loading my stuff and then we are going to leave."

"You're coming? Holy shit, but what about—"

"Never mind her, it wasn't working out anyways. But then again, if you had been around for the last few months you would know that." He finishes loading his stuff, parks his truck on the street and gets in. "Let's roll." he says.

"Nick, I just want to say—"

"Stop talking. Go, please, before I change my mind." I put the car in drive and we leave this city for good.

"So where the hell are we going?"

"I owe someone a favor."

It's the twilight hour right before dawn breaks. We sit inside my little convertible with the top up, hunkering down in our seats discussing our plans. A thick dark blue hue blankets the neighborhood. A neighborhood nestled in bed in those final precious moments just before the day's alarm clock sounds. A neighborhood that is silent, waiting in anticipation to come to life, save for us.

"Here is how it goes down."

"This is insane. You're going to get us arrested."

"Shut up. Maybe you don't understand, but I have to do this."

"I already said I'm in, I was merely voicing my opinion."

"Well, I need you to keep it to yourself before I lose my nerve."

"Okay, you got it, I'll shut up. So what's the plan?"

"Deb goes to work at 6, and Nigel goes at 7:30. However, she comes outside to start her car at 5:30. When she starts her car, you creep up from around the garage and lock her keys in her car while it's running. She keeps a spare set hidden somewhere outside. We watch where she goes to get the spare set. She unlocks her car door, puts it back, and leaves. We wait an hour. Nigel goes to work. They don't have any pets or kids. It's simple. I go in, steal the urn, and then we leave."

"What if she doesn't put the spare key back?"

"She will."

"What if they have a security system?"

"Stop worrying, if you worry about something going wrong, it will." I glance down at the small digital clock on the dash, it's 5:15. On the second story of the house a bedroom light flicks on. "Like clockwork," I think out loud.

Following suit, the living room lights come to life, and then the kitchen lights. Fifteen minutes later Deb comes walking outside in red slippers and a maroon bathrobe. She starts her car and goes back inside the house, paying no attention to our parked car.

"Show time."

"Wish me luck."

"Good luck," I say, playfully punching him in the arm.

Nick moves slowly out of the car, creeping along the hedges bordering the driveway, keeping low. He crouches on the ground next to the passenger door of Deb's car and looks back at me. I see my aunt's bathroom light go on and flick my lighter once, signaling that the coast is clear. He opens the door, hits the automatic lock button and closes it quietly. Just as he closes the car door, Nigel walks out the front door to load his tools into his truck. He is an hour early. Nick flinches when the door slams and rolls to the right, sliding underneath Nigel's truck. Nigel drops the big black tool bag into the bed of the truck, gets into the driver's seat, and starts the engine. We didn't plan for this. I watch helplessly as his reverse lights come on and he begins to slowly back out of his driveway. In a few seconds he will be staring at Nick lying in his driveway. Unless Nick chances being run over by rolling out the side and under my aunt's running car.

I hold my breath. The truck's brake lights come on and the reverse lights shut off. The driver's door swings open and Nigel gets out and goes back inside the house. Nick shimmies out and slides underneath Deb's car. A few minutes later, Nigel leaves without noticing my car. Then Deb comes out and begins to fight with her locked car doors. She retrieves her spare keys from a fake rock in the garden, unlocks her car, and returns the keys to their hiding place. As soon as she's inside the house Nick books it back to the car.

"I thought you said he goes to work at 7:30?"

I shrug my shoulders with a smirk. "He usually does." Nick calls me an asshole under his breath as Deb pulls out of the driveway, leaving for the day.

"Now it's my turn," I say, unbuckling my seat belt and opening the car door once Deb is out of view. I'm in and out of her house in less than five minutes. Back in my car, I sit with my grandmother's ashes in my lap.

"I can't believe I just did this."

"We should go," Nick says, giving me strange looks from the corner of his eye.

"What?"

"Dude, your grandma would get the biggest kick out of this."

"I know."

"Where are we headed with this thing anyway?"

"Please, she's still my grandma."

"Sorry. So where are we going?"

"To take her home," I say, lighting a cigarette.

3

"Do you think he is up?"

"Nick, I don't care if he is up. The point is to reunite them; it doesn't matter if he knows who did it."

The blazing orange sun illuminates the horizon behind my grandfather's house with deep reds and fringes of pink. I don't think he is awake yet; the giant house is dark and silent. He has been sleeping later and later since Grandma died. One cautious step at a time I approach the front door with the urn clasped between my hands. Like a weary traveler at the end of his pilgrimage, I kneel before the concrete steps. As soon as the rough cement scrapes the bottom of the porcelain urn I take my hands off it. I close my eyes, bowing my head in memorial.

"Hi Grandma, it's me. I haven't been the best person lately. I don't think you would be proud of me. I've committed crimes, almost drank myself to death, hell, I even cussed at a priest. I don't know what you wanted me to make of myself. And I don't know why you left me such an inheritance, but Grandpa told me that this is my chance. And for once I think it just might be my chance. But before I begin this odyssey, I felt you deserved to be home, with your husband. I'll see you soon." I kiss the tip of my thumb and press it on the urn.

My stomach pangs as I walk down the driveway for the last time. Saying goodbye is never easy. Nick has the car idling at the road. I get in the passenger seat and wipe the remaining tears from my eyes.

"Are you ready for this?" he asks over the high pitched whine of the ragtop's roof motor. The damp morning air washes over us, refreshing us for the journey ahead.

Less than an hour later we put the pedal to the floor with the top down. Warm wind whips our hair and flings our cigarette ashes all over the car. Considering we have just committed a felony break-in with possible charges for stealing the dead, it's in our best interests to get out of this state as fast as we can. Nick figures if we double the speed limit it will seem as if we left at five rather than eight, giving us a rock solid alibi. An alibi that we won't need, because by then I will be dead.

"I know what direction we are heading, but where are we actually going?" Nick says, breaking my train of thought.

"We're heading where any two young guys about to embark on a mystical journey should begin." I stand up in my seat with my hands over my head letting the wind take me. "Where the American dream first took root, poisoning this land with its rot!" I point eastward. "We're going to New York City!"

"Sit down man, we're doing almost 90! You're going to get yourself killed!"

He grabs the collar of my shirt and pulls me down into my seat.

"It's a good day to die, Nick."

Our tires crunch along the gravel driveway of our first stop. I still can't believe how fast we got here. Nick stands up in the driver's seat, sticking his head out of the top of the convertible. Milliseconds later he slumps back into his seat thumping his head against the seat rest, looking uninspired.

"What is that?" His tone is drone-like, as if I had just dragged him to the world's most boring lecture.

"A giant duck."

"I know what it is, what's inside it?"

"A store that sells duck stuff!" I shout, jumping over the door out of the car. "Quick, come get a picture of me in front of it!"

Nick grabs the camera from the backseat and walks toward the duck.

"One picture, then we're leaving."

"Awe, come on, this is our first major stop. A milestone. Plus I want to buy some touristy duck crap."

"Major? The Empire State Building, that's major. This is a giant-ass duck."

"Fine."

I smile big and he snaps a few shots of me in front of the duck. Then we get back into the car and continue our journey towards the city that never sleeps.

 5

We approach the Hotel Chelsea at noon. Check-in probably isn't until three but I convince Nick that we can sweet talk or even bribe them to let us in early. This will give us a chance to shower and change, drop off our gear, and decompress from the drive. It's also because of my own sheer giddiness. I have wanted to stay at the Chelsea since I was fifteen. For me it is more than a hotel, it's a bohemian Mecca. The Chelsea was a home to most, if not all of my heroes. Johnny Thunders, Mark Twain, Charles Bukowski, Iggy Pop, and Uma Thurman, just to name a few. This hotel defines what it is to live rock and roll. A statue to everything that is pure and untainted by corporate greed. This is a dream come true. But, it also is the place where junky rock star Sid Vicious killed his girlfriend Nancy Spungent, and I can't help draw some parallels between them and Kat and me.

Our first shock comes when we pull up to the curb in front of the hotel and there is only one spot to park. I thought it would have been kept clear for the valet, taxis, and limousines. We wait for a couple of minutes.

"You said this place has valet."

"I thought they did."

"Well where is everyone?"

"Fuck if I know, come on." We put the top up and get out, looking up and down the busy sidewalk. "Check in first and then grab the bags?"

"Sure."

We head to the front entrance, but still haven't seen anyone, not even a bellhop. The second shock comes as I slam face-first into the firm glass of a locked door.

"Fuck." I stagger back and then try the door again; it's definitely locked. "Are they closed?"

"Uh, dude, open your eyes."

In my star-struck awe I missed a small white note taped inside the glass. *The Hotel Chelsea is temporarily closed. We apologize for any inconvenience. Thank you.*

"You've got to be kidding me. We just fucking drove six hours to stay at this place and it's closed?" I start looking to the crowds of New Yorkers passing by us for guidance. "Hey, does anyone know why this place is closed?"

People walk right through me. Cell phones pushed up against their ears and glowing Bluetooth's illuminating the sides of their heads. They all look the same and use any excuse to ignore the psychotic guy flipping out about a hotel. Hell, they are probably so used to freaks like me they don't even hear my cries.

"Come on let's get out of here, we'll just find another hotel."

Find another hotel? Was he crazy? There is no other hotel. I've waited my entire life to be presented with this opportunity only to find it fucking disarmed by a god-damned note from management? Bullshit.

"No."

"No? And what do you plan on doing? Breaking in? Come on there are plenty of hotels in New York."

"No. They're not like this one. I've waited my whole life to stay at this place and nothing is going to stand in my way."

"It's locked. It's a no go, comprende?"

"Look, there are still people living here. It has permanent residents. We wait until—"

"Absolutely not!"

"This is nonnegotiable, you signed up for this. We are two guys in search of the American dream—"

"You know what? Fine. You're the captain of this ship. But if you get us arrested so help me God."

"It will be fine, trust me."

"Famous last words," he scoffs, rolling his eyes.

It took three hours of hanging around smoking and loitering in front of, beside, and across the street from the Chelsea to get a break. It comes so fast we almost miss it. Out of the corner of my eye I catch the door opening. An older woman in a purple dress and a bright red feathered hat comes walking out. She is so small it barely opens. We have only a fraction of a second to react and we are too far away to do so without running and blowing our cover. *Shit.* Then I look to my feet and notice a small rock right at the tip of my black converse. *Once in a lifetime.* The thought flashes through my cancerous brain, panicking me. I kick the pebble towards the door. It skips three times along the concrete sidewalk bouncing in between the legs of a businessman with exceptionally greasy hair. My heart stops as the rock skips again, sails upward on its last bounce and then right over the small lip and into the Chelsea. The door clicks shut and the small woman slides a narrow Virginia Slim out of a metal cigarette case and sticks it in her crinkled, pursed lips. Before she can make another move I hold a lighter under it and she puffs the cherry to life.

"Well aren't you a darling," she rasps through a larynx coated in decades of nicotine.

"My pleasure," I say, gripping the door handle. The amended plan was to tell her we forgot our keys and hope she was senile enough to not remember never seeing us. And then it happened. The door slips open in my grip. Giving her one last smile and a slight bow I steer my eyes to the bottom of the door frame. Right in the crack is my pebble, it slid in just enough. We walk over the threshold into a world I never thought I would see. Blindingly bright, artwork adorns every wall.

"You are the luckiest son of a bitch—" Nick is interrupted by a middle-aged man standing at the front desk. He is business casual with a black sports coat and tan khakis. His round thin metal framed glass are balanced so far down the tip of his angular nose they look as if they might tumble to the desk without so much as a sneeze.

"Can I help you two?"

"Uh …" I begin to stutter, unprepared for a front desk clerk to be in a building closed to the general public.

"Oh, you two must be with the new management team," he sneers.

"Uh … yeah, why is there a problem?"

"Yeah, tell Vargas the residents want their trash taken out. Probably should have thought about that before the entire housekeeping staff was terminated."

"Absolutely, my good man, this sounds like an issue we can directly assist with." My bullshit gear shifts into drive automatically. Putting my elbows on the countertop I lean in and hush my voice to stress the importance of what I am about to say. "Hey, Vargas didn't by any chance leave a couple sets of keys behind did he?"

The clerk scrunches up his nose. "I don't think so, that's not really how things work here, but let me check in the office." He disappears through a door behind the desk.

"What the fuck are you doing?" Beads of sweat are forming along the top of Nick's furrowed brow.

"I told you, we didn't come all this way to not stay here."

"We're going to jail," he whispers.

"No, we're not. Now wipe your forehead, control your pit stains, and be cool."

The clerk returns with a small ring of keys. "I guess so, because I don't remember seeing these around." He slides the keys to the bohemian kingdom across the desk. I feel a surge of raw energy as I pick them up. Like the spirits of a thousand dead artists entering my soul through my fingertips. If only sex was this good. I try not to show any signs of enthusiasm while holding them, the key right now is calm and cool.

"You haven't heard from Vargas at all have you?" I ask. "We've been planning this for months but emails went silent about two weeks ago."

"No, but I can call for you—"

"That won't be necessary." I slide my phone out of my pocket, pretending to look at it in a bid to prevent our ruse from coming apart. "I can call him while he unloads."

"Her."

"What?"

"You can call her, right? You do know Vargas is a woman, don't you?"

Fuck. The ruse is coming apart.

"He didn't say that!" Nick interjects, startling me a bit. "Do you hear what he is suggesting?" Nick is talking as loud as he can without shouting. "Call Vargas right now, tell her to add another department to the housekeeping layoffs. We can handle the damn door without this pompous—"

"Wait, stop, I'm sorry. Please sirs, you misunderstood me. You can unload whatever you brought for Vargas in the loading dock and feel free to choose any empty room to accommodate yourselves until you meet with her."

"Calm down," I tell Nick. "Thank you sir, I'm sorry about him. We had an aggressive pilot and he is still edgy from the flight."

"Not a problem, it was never my intention to correct," he pauses and begins eyeing us up and down. If I didn't have the keys in my hand, I would swear he knew the truth. "As you have most likely been informed, all of the guest room doors have been painted white. Here are the two masters you will need to access them."

"Thank you, sir." I slide five crisp hundred dollar bills across the granite desk to him. His eyes widen and he slips the money into the breast pocket of his sport coat.

"Harold is the name and the pleasure is all mine." With a bow he returns to his newspaper.

If our story didn't convince him, the money did, which worked out perfect because the stay in the suite we wanted to book would have tripled that price. We head outside to the car to retrieve our bags from the trunk.

"Give me a cigarette," Nick sighs, wiping the sweat off his forehead with the front of his black shirt.

"Damn, you okay?" I light two cigarettes and hand him one.

"I can't believe that worked. You're a fucking maniac."

I pretend to breathe on my fingernails and wipe them on my shirt. "All in a day's work."

We don't bother driving around to the loading dock, since Harold has already given us the keys. We lug our bags inside, past the front desk, and to the stairs. Harold is nowhere in sight, so we feel a little bit less guarded. The stairs look exactly like they did in my dreams. Beautiful rolling curls carved just below the dark, glossy banister. They wind upwards, as far as we can see. Original artwork, donated by previous tenants, is along the walls and capping every bend.

"Once we go up there … and go inside one of those rooms … there is no turning back. We're all in. We can go to jail for this," Nick says.

Nick is staring up the first flight, his eyes locked on a Larry Rivers painting, *Fashion and The Birds; Blue Dress*. But he doesn't see the same image I do. I can tell his mind's eye paints a different portrait, one of us in orange jumpsuits. Growing up we had been bad. Not Macaulay Culkin in *The*

Good Son bad, more like *Dennis the Menace* bad. But this was a whole new dimension of wrong for both of us.

"I was all in when I got in the car. Besides, is this any worse than stealing my dead grandmother's ashes?"

Silence. I didn't expect an answer. I'm not sure what I expect. He's not going to run from the hotel, keys in hand, and steal my car. So there really is nothing to worry about. But I didn't expect him to do what he does. Without a word, or even a facial expression, he hoists his black duffle bag strap over his shoulder, looks at his feet, and initiates our ascent into rock and roll royalty.

Three floors up we halt our climb and begin wandering the halls to select a room. The third door we unlock has minimalist postmodern décor. Everything from the coarse rug to the bedding is a mix of drab grays and violent whites. No fridge or kitchenette. No dressers or bookshelves. No television. It is just a large open room with a giant bed in the center, several chairs of very abstract shapes and sizes, a balcony, and a bathroom. The bathtub looks like a giant grey soup bowl with a well spigot in it. The shower walls and floor are a shiny black marble and there is a single rainfall showerhead hanging in the center, and no curtain or walls. This is by far the most bizarre room I have ever been in. It looks to be crafted from the mind of Andy Warhol himself. But something about this room brings a strange feeling of comfort, peace. No distractions for my mind to run amok with.

Where there might have once been the entrance to the kitchen or a window, now hangs a black and white striped silk curtain. I walk inside and drop my bag. I stroll over to the curtain and slide it open to reveal an elegant wood fireplace painted matte black. The fireplace is framed with grey bricks, not that it ever could have been used on the third floor without a chimney.

"I'm home."

"Of course you are," Nick says, dropping his bag on the floor next to mine. "Better call for some extra pillows."

This statement causes me to look upon him with confusion. "I'm so uncomfortable staying in this hotel right now. If we get busted I'd like to at least be in the same room so we have a chance at getting the fuck out of here."

"Fine."

"This room is kind of eerie. Like living in an Apple store."

I charge across the room diving into the bed and wrapping myself up in the cloud-like blankets.

"I love it!"

"You've been standing on that balcony staring at the city, smoking, for almost two hours."

"So what?"

"Dude, there is nothing to do in here. And you've almost smoked two packs of cigarettes. Let's get out, we came here to see the sights, live the life and chase the American Dream. Not lie around some creepy hotel."

"What do you propose we do?" I say, ignoring his comments about the room.

"Let's walk down Times Square, go to China Town. We have the whole of New York at our disposal, let's go."

I've never seen him this way, giddy. Well, as giddy as Nick gets.

"I have always wanted to catch a show at CBGB's, we can start there," I say, looking at my phone. It's almost 8 p.m. "We can have a drink, see what's playing, and go from there."

When we get to CBGB's, it's the Chelsea all over again. Instead of being met with earth quaking music and a line out the door, we find a deserted street and a closed metal shutter. The canopy with the club's name has been taken down, leaving a skeletal appearance where the frame still hangs. Scrawled in different colors of marker on the shutter barring our entrance are the names of hundreds of bands. Bands that have been climbing the stage inside since the 70s. Some getting their start, while others perpetuated the legend of CBGB's after their own meteoric rise to stardom. I punch the shutter as hard as I can, doing more damage to my fist than the door.

"What the fuck?" I shout, trying to wave away the stinging pain in my fist.

"Dude, have you heard of the Internet? Did you research anything you wanted to do before we got in the car? Because so far you're batting zero."

"How the fuck was I supposed to know? I knew some of the things I wanted to do, but apparently, fate has different plans. Fuck!" I scream, slamming the bottom of my other fist into the shutter and instantly it stings. "Why can't anything ever work out?"

Putting both my aching hands on the entrance, I lean my head in, banging it on the shutter, and then slide down to my knees. Bowing my head, I try not to cry, not letting this temper tantrum take full control.

"Oui, it's a damn shame, mate!"

The voice from behind grabs me through a thick Australian accent. I rise, doing an about face to meet the

184

stranger. What stands before me takes the words right out of my mouth. He is about 6'5" counting his hair. It is hard to find a bare patch of skin in the cascading tattoos that go all the way from his knuckles to his ears. Tattoos can even be seen in the holes ripped in his faded denim jeans. His black wife-beater has a picture of a bloody heart with deer antlers, and I have yet to figure out how he keeps the lime green Mohawk standing so straight.

"I hear they're gonna turn this into a damn clothier … some type of men's fucking warehouse—" He slams his fist into the metal shutter so hard his knuckles crack. "Corporate pig fuckers!" He steps too close to me, way inside my comfort zone. "You look about as pissed as I am right now, what's your name, mate?"

"Dave." Before I can flinch he grabs my hand and pulls me in for a strong hug.

"Oui Dave, put her there, good to fucking meetchya. Names Spyder, of The Deer Hearts."

"The Deer Hearts?" I scrunch my face and look at Nick, he shrugs.

"Australia's finest in punk, rock mate! We're making our North American debut in a month and wanted to do some sightseeing before we get to recording. Aye, Lauren, get these guys a fucking CD!"

A female version of Spyder returns with two CDs and two black wife-beaters identical to Spyder's. Nick and I share a glance when we get a closer look at her. Her hair is jet black and teased into a rats nest. Everything else, the ripped jeans, tattoos, and wife beater, looked taken from Spyder's wardrobe.

"Jesus Christ, is this his girlfriend or sister?" Nick whispers to me.

I shrug, pull my t-shirt off, drop it to the sidewalk, and put on the band shirt.

"Oui, that's the fucking spirit, mate. Now what do ya say to a pint or ten? Come tour the ole NY of C with us?"

I look to Nick, now standing behind Spyder, shaking his head no. "Yeah, that'll be great. Where's your car?" I say, in direct defiance of my companion.

"Car? I'm a fucking rock star! My limo is parked around the corner."

Inside the limousine is a spoiled adult's playground. A full bar, complete with the mirror behind the bottles, displays every kind of alcohol imaginable. On the left side, instead of a window, is a 40-inch plasma screen. And if we get hungry, the seats lift up revealing a refrigerator stocked with food.

"I say, if you're gonna party, why go to clubs? Fuck clubs, they ruin the scene. Take the party on the road." Spyder's accent is starting to grate on my nerves. He's cool and all, just a bit overbearing. I raise my glass in a mock toast, which he and Lauren take seriously.

"I'll drink to that." I smirk, before downing a half glass of scotch.

"Hold up," he says, grabbing the empty glass from my hand. "I've got something special."

Spyder pulls a small black leather bag from the floor by the TV and unzips it, producing a plastic bag of white powder. Then he pulls out a switchblade and flicks it open. The handle of the switchblade looks to be made of ivory and has a picture of Mother Mary carved into it. Carefully he sticks the knife into the bag and then shoves the blade underneath my nose.

"Man up!" he shouts, his face twitching with madness. Without glancing for Nick's approval I plug one nostril and snort the length of the blade. Then I scream, but I don't know how long I scream for. It's great, like a shot of liquid Superman injected straight into my balls.

"Quick, drain this," he shoves a glass of scotch in my face and I slam it. "One to bring you up and one to bring you down."

Spyder cheers before doing a line off of his knife. "Awe, she kissed ya mate."

He points to my bleeding upper lip.

We cruise the city for almost an hour before getting bored. Nick stays quiet, sticking to beer and flipping through channels on the TV. Lauren hops on his lap a few times, without any protests from her boyfriend, but he denies her advances. Spyder and I keep drinking, doing lines, and swapping tales. Then I bring up the Chelsea Hotel. I tell him all about our impromptu invasion of the punk paradise. In an instant, his buzz is gone and he's leaning forward in his seat, captivated by my tale. He keeps fishing into his bag and popping pills like they're Spree. As I finish, he produces his coke knife again. Squinting my eyes shut I snort the line off the blade and slam a shot of tequila.

"You're staying at the fucking Chelsea?"

"Yeah," I choke out, lighting a cigarette to get the taste of tequila out of my mouth.

"Fucking-a, then we're staying at the Chelsea," he says, dialing his cell phone. I've lost his attention for the moment. Whoever is on the phone suddenly takes precedence. "Oui, yeah, it's me. Yeah, get the crew together, we're having a party at the Chelsea. Nah, it's open to us, yeah, I met someone." He hangs up the phone and tosses it on the seat between us. Then he puts down the mirror behind the bar, revealing the back of the driver's head. "Driver, Chelsea Hotel, please."

My head is starting to spin, the concoction of coke and booze makes me loopy. I try to stand in the moving vehicle but fall to the floor in front of Nick. He pulls me on to the seat next to him.

"What do you think you are doing? We can't take these maniacs back there," he's holding me by my shirt and breathing beer stink down my throat.

"Trust me," I grin in my drug addled state. "And have a few more drinks."

I pull away from him and crawl back to my seat next to Spyder.

On the ride back to the hotel, Spyder insists that our chance meeting in the street was fate, proven to him undeniably by the fact that the Chelsea was closed when he tried to book a room and now we're somehow staying there. As he blabs on, Nick's words begin to sink in. Maybe inviting this maniac and his band mates to a hotel we have no business staying in isn't such a hot idea. But Spyder seems like a guy who is used to getting what he wants, and so I push back every ounce of good judgment trying to break through my drug induced haze and take them back to the hotel.

"We've got to distract him," Nick murmurs while Spyder and Lauren tour our room.

"I know, follow my lead." I walk over and put an arm around Spyder. "Hey, Nick and I were really hoping to see some of the sights tonight. Empire State Building, Statue of Liberty, maybe the World Trade Center Memorial. How about we hook up and party later?"

"Oh yeah, my thought exactly," he bellows through his barely decipherable accent. "It'll take some time to get everyone together anyways. But first a drink to the chance meeting of good friends."

He raises a gaudy diamond encrusted flask and then takes a long gulp before shoving the flask into my hand.

"To good people," I say, taking a long drink.

When I come out of my blackout, we're in the loading dock of the Chelsea surrounded by people. My head is pounding, the voices of the crowd blending into one loud mush of talk. I close my eyes and grab my temples, doubling over onto the ground.

"Hey man, you alright?" Spyder's twisted grin is the first thing I see when I open my eyes. "Here take these, you'll feel better."

He hands me a couple of colorful pills and his signature bedazzled flask. Everyone around me is carrying shit and I don't see Nick. Spyder keeps barking orders and telling people room numbers. In the time between our toast and now, I have obviously failed in keeping this party from reaching the hotel. A carnival of freaks flood into the loading dock of the Chelsea. I may have fucked up.

"What about sight-seeing and the tourist shit?" I ask Spyder.

"Quit fucking around mate, we did everything this city has to offer and have pictures to prove it. Now it's time to get our punk rock on." His speech is slurred and half his face looks like it isn't moving. If I didn't know better I would think he was having a stroke. "Here, your nose is bleeding." He hands me the crusty red hanky dangling out of his pocket.

I put the hanky to my nose and pop the pills, washing them down with whatever is in his bottle. Better to be numb than face these consequences.

8

I'm lying in the corner of a hotel room, wound up in a ball of blankets. I look around. The hardwood floor is covered in Oriental rugs. The furniture is dark leather and mahogany bookshelves line the walls. This isn't our suite. The time on the digital clock, which dangles upside down from an overturned dresser, reads 6:30 p.m. I lift myself up, bracing against the dresser. My head is screaming. Taking a couple steps, the cartilage in my knees turns to Jell-O and I fall face first to the floor. I barely catch myself on the couch, which I now notice is turned on its side. Empty cans and bottles litter every flat surface my eyes scan. Crawling on my hands and knees, I drag myself towards an open door that leads to a toilet. I crawl into the bathroom and stand to piss, bracing myself on the sink.

"Uuuuugghhh ..."

The noise startles me but doesn't interrupt my peeing. I can see the top of Nick's recently shaved head poking out of a wad of blankets in the claw foot bathtub.

"You alive?" I say, finishing my pee and leaning down on the edge of the tub.

"Yeah ... It's fucking cold in here," he groans, wrapping up tighter in the blankets.

"What? No it's not."

"Easy for you to say, I'm sleeping in two inches of water."

"Leaky shower head?"

"No, the last thing I remember is wanting to take a bath. But I fell asleep and someone shoved blankets and pillows on me." He pushes the blankets out of the tub and they make a sopping wet thunk as they hit the floor.

"They shaved your head, too, baldy." I rub his head playfully. "But seriously, we should really leave."

The severity of the situation is setting in. It was innocent enough when it was just us sleeping here. But not now, with the freak show we paraded through here last night. Enough drugs and alcohol to make an army see God by showing them hell. This, well this, is a problem.

Nick stands and steps out of the tub, water splashing everywhere. We walk out into the living room and stop. Not one piece of furniture is in its original place. Half-eaten fruit baskets are smashed about, banana and apple guts mashed into the rugs and smeared on the walls. Broken glass, crumpled beer cans, and empty Jack Daniels bottles are strewn almost decoratively.

"What the fuck did we do?"

We walk across the living room to the only clear spot. The coffee table has had all of its legs broken off and the top of it is propped up on a milk crate. In the center is a single photo album and next to it is a handwritten note with Spyder's switchblade stuck in it.

You two are Norse Gods. I'll probably lose my visa after a party like that. If you're ever in Melbourne look us up – S&L

"This may be a clue."

I flip open the photo album, page after page of pictures of the four of us at every monument and national landmark in the city. Pictures of us drinking in clubs, riding in taxis.

"Do you remember any of this?" I ask him.

Without answering he dashes into the kitchen pulling his leather jacket down from the top of the refrigerator. A cascade of vegetables and crushed beer cans come crashing down around him. He slides his cell out of his jacket pocket.

"It's Wednesday …"

"So?" I say, kicking an empty bottle across the living room floor.

"We got here Monday afternoon."

Silence. I wrench Spyder's switchblade out of the table and crumple the note, tossing it on the floor.

"Go back to our room and get our shit, we've got to go, I'll meet you down stairs."

Nick rushes out and I start rummaging through the garbage. Grabbing a plastic bag from the floor I shove anything incriminating or traceable I can find, but the photo album and some credit card receipts are the only things I see. In my frenzied ransacking I come across a half pack of cigarettes and light one up. Then with a bulging bag of wrinkled papers and garbage I sprint for the door to meet up with Nick. Halfway there a jagged piece of glass pierces the bottom of my foot and sends me reeling to the floor. I slide through a pile of garbage, whiskey bottles and more broken glass and come to rest on the floor, half inside the coat closet. Directly in front of my face is a small leather toiletry bag, distracting me from the hot pulsing pain of my bleeding foot. I reach for the bag and pull it towards me, slide the center zipper open and behold an unbelievable sight. It's Spyder's drug bag. The one he had been lugging around in the limo for our entire three-day binge. It's so packed with painkillers and prescription drugs that the sides are swollen and the zipper is hard to get closed. I sling it over my shoulder, limping back to our original room.

When I get down two flights of stairs, Nick is already locking the door to our suite, strained with both of our bags. He hustles to the staircase and joins me in the descent to freedom.

"So we have to leave New York I take it?" He huffs, out of breath and hung-over.

195

"Yeah, this is a catastrophe; I can't believe things got so out of hand."

My foot throbs with pain, like my head and every other part of my body. I stagger down the last step, catching myself on the hand railing. I squint my eyes shut as if it will help. When I open my eyes, I see Nick frozen in fear. Standing in front of us is the old woman I held the door for a few days ago. She is coming in from a cigarette. She is the only thing impeding our escape.

"Are you okay?" she croaks.

Nick and I look at each other in shock. In our hasty departure we hadn't quite grasped what we look like. Nick is in a rented tuxedo, an undone bowtie hanging from his neck and the cummerbund missing. The shiny black shoes that usually accompany a tux are gone, replaced by black boots. His left eye socket is bruised black and blue, the outer most edges singed with a jaundice yellow brown. Me? I'm in a black t-shirt and grey sports coat. There is a cigarette dangling from my dry cracked lips. I'm not wearing any pants. And a trail of single bloody footprints comes all the way down the stairs.

"Yeah, of course we are okay. What in the blazing name of hell would give you any other idea? We're just minding our damn business down here deciding where to get coffee."

Crazy is the best approach. Offend her, get her to go away.

"You're bleeding," she says. "Bad. Let me get Harold, he'll have some bandages in his desk." The little woman steps behind the counter and disappears into Harold's office door.

Nick and I don't exchange glances, we bolt. No hesitation, no looking back. A few seconds later we're starting the car. Nick floors it, pulling out into traffic and putting The Chelsea at our backs.

"What the fuck happened?" he says, smoking a cigarette, hands shaking.

"We over-stayed our welcome in New York," I pull out Spyder's switchblade and flick it open, slice into the bottom of my foot and dig out the mammoth hunk of glass.

"What the hell are you doing?" Nick shouts. Blood runs all over the seat. Without saying anything I withdraw the sizable chunk of glass from my foot and toss it out the window. "You walked down all those flights with that stuck in your foot?" He looks exhausted from this ordeal.

"Yeah, fuck," I cough, fighting nausea, and then breath a heavy sigh of relief as the bleeding of my foot slows. "I don't know what happened back there. We'll have to consult the photo album. After the toast, everything kind of goes black." I sniffle, and begin rubbing my eyes. "Just drive man. I'm starving."

"Yeah, I'm not stopping for eats until we're off the island."

"That's fine."

But we don't stop for food when we get off of the island. We don't put the top down or turn the radio on. We just drive, in silent reflection of our debauchery. Maybe it was out of fear or anger but when Nick hit Interstate 80, he floors it. My stomach is a knotted wreck and the world is still spinning, even with my eyes closed. I roll my window down to let some fresh air into the car. It feels nice on my face, cool. Probably the only thing keeping me from puking. I lean my head against the seat, thinking of the past few days, trying to remember. As the wind tosses and tussles my hair, my mind drifts back to Kat, when we were on the roller coaster. And then I fall asleep.

When I wake up quite some time has passed. In fact, I've been sleeping for nine hours. The car isn't moving. My stomach wails and moans. I open the car door and throw up in a parking lot. The vomit is a collage of blood, purple and brown. I can even make out some mushy pills in the mixture. Sweaty and nauseas, I look to the empty driver's seat and try to figure out my whereabouts. I see Nick walking across the parking lot of a Burger King with two bags and a drink tray.

"Awe fuck, you couldn't make it to a bathroom?"

"Man, I don't feel right." I pull a pair of jeans out of the back, sidestep my puddle of regurgitation, and put them on.

"You shouldn't feel right, with all of the drugs and alcohol you've ingested. Come on, let's eat."

Barefoot and limping I follow him to a picnic table along the highway in front of the restaurant. He hands me a bag of food and a drink.

"Hope you don't mind, it's a chicken club with a large fry and Coke."

I shake my head and unwrap the food on the table in front of me. It looks disgusting; soggy bun, bacon that could be plastic, and a block of chicken so processed and deep fried it might as well be a sponge. I take small bites and chew them slow.

"We need to talk about what happened," Nick says between handfuls of fries. "I've seen some shit, but I can't handle partying like that. What the fuck happened to you back there?" He stops eating and waits for an explanation.

"I … I don't know."

"You don't know?" he chuckles. "You, who never even smoked pot, begin a vacation in New York City by shoving more cocaine up your nose than that fucked up rocker and his girlfriend?"

"I … I …"

"You and Spyder were popping pills like Pez. Drinking, snorting, and blathering on about maintaining some level of sobriety. Do you even remember fucking Lauren?"

"What?"

"Yeah, he caught you checking her out and told you to have a go. And you did it, right there on the floor in the middle of the party at the Chelsea."

I put my head into my hands and rub my face. It's clear he remembers more of what happened than me. But why the admonishment?

"I know what I did was wrong, but what do you want? An apology? What happened, I can't change any of it."

"That's not what I mean," he pops the last bite of his sandwich into his mouth and washes it down with a sip of Coke. "I don't know the guy I spent the last few days with, and I'm not sure I like him. We want to enjoy this trip, experience it to the fullest, but we also want to survive. And if we want to do all of this we need a better plan, not an exact itinerary, but at least some direction." He lights two cigarettes and then hands me one. "So captain, where are we going?"

"That depends, where are we?"

"Toledo, Ohio."

"We missed the Rock and Roll Hall of Fame." I look up to the sky, and then to a passing Buick, and then back to Nick. "What about Mount Rushmore? I've always wanted to see that."

"That sounds fun. You want to go straight there? Or cut through Chicago and see the Sears Tower?"

I drum my fingers on the table for a second. "I don't know. A part of me has seen enough of big cities for a bit."

"Agreed. Mount Rushmore it is."

It's a long ways from Ohio to Iowa. I couldn't tell you what town we're in, names stopped mattering after Indiana. After almost 10 hours, every passing sign starts to look like the same green blur. In desperate need of a break from the highway we stop at the first hotel we see in Iowa. It doesn't happen until we drive almost completely across the damn state, but more hungry than tired, we don't even unpack, we walk to the closest bar, a place called Jack's. Comfort food, chicken wings and burgers, is just what we need. We lounge around this dump for hours, chatting with whoever will talk. But, the locals in this backwoods town treat us like we have the plague.

I stare at the thick head of foam on my third pint of Guinness, losing myself in it's froth. Nick is across the bar hitting on a leggy blonde while I drink alone, unwinding from a long drive. I take a good, long sip of beer and set the glass on the bar. That's the precise moment she comes in, her perfect body swaying up to the bar right next to me. I don't look as she orders a vodka tonic. My heart races, and I continue drinking my beer, and taking shaky drags off my cigarette. She has the most beautiful black hair I've ever seen. It's the kind that is so black it's blue.

"Excuse me, do you have the time?" she says. Trying not to look in her direction, I don't realize she is talking to me. She puts her hand on mine and gives it a small squeeze. It sends a shock up my arm, jolting me like I licked a nine volt battery.

"Oh, you mean me?" That's what I say, instantly regretting it.

"Yeah, I mean you love. Do you have the time?"

"No, I don't wear a watch." Again, feeling shame.

"Too bad," she says with a smirk, taking her vodka and walking away.

The bartender, a middle-aged man in a red flannel shirt and jeans that fit him properly 20 years ago, comes to my end of the bar.

"Wow, she don't talk to many folk in here. If you're asking me, I'd say she likes you." He smirks and winks his eye.

"Well, I wasn't," I say, looking back down at my beer. I try to will him away before I do something I will regret for the rest of this trip.

"Fine." The universe answers my prayers and sends him back to polishing wine glasses at the other end of the bar.

But whatever spark that bartender noticed between us was there. In truth, just seeing her was a flood of emotion I haven't felt since being with Katrina. In an instant, I dreamt of knowing her. Knowing what we could never have because of my disease. A lifetime unfolds in my head as if to appease my convoluted sense of love. She and I are moving into an apartment, a small duplex on the right side of town. Picking out furniture at IKEA, and spending hours deciding on the paint samples spread out across the dining room table. We go to the pound and adopt a dog, a small Jack-Russell with a slight limp. On the way out I point to a Doberman with a red rocket between his legs and she giggles, taking me by the arm. Flash forward and we're walking down the aisle, pledging our eternal love in front of our families. More years pass and we're in the maternity ward, she's holding our baby and my parents are congratulating us. This is what every guy pictures when they know they are in love with someone the second they see them. But the lump of cancerous flesh spreading throughout my brain stops me. I have to be content only with dreams.

Taking another sip of my beer I look back to her. Watching is the only thing I will allow myself to do. A police officer takes the seat next to her. My seat. He puts his arm around her and kisses her neck as she squirms in his grasp. I take another sip, getting lost in my beer foam again.

"Hey, I'm going to head out to our car with Cindy for a bit," Nick says from behind, startling me and breaking my thought.

"Alright, I'll be right here."

"Yeah I bet," he leans in closer to my ear. "Too bad about officer fuck face over there. I saw the way you two looked at each other." He smiles at me.

"Get out of here; go have fun fucking whatever the hell her name is. I'll meet you back at the car in a couple hours."

"Okay, catch ya later."

The blond leads him out of the bar. It's fine, he deserves it. I look down and see a glop of red floating on top of the white foam in my drink. I reach in with two fingers and try to fish it out as a drop of red hits the back of my hand. Quickly I raise a napkin to my nose as a steady stream starts to drizzle out.

"Bartender!" I shout, as the blood soaks through the napkin and runs down my hand.

"Yeah?" he says, without even looking up.

"Where the hell is the bathroom?"

"Listen buddy, don't go barking orders ... Holy shit, are you all right?"

"The bathroom?" I ask.

"Down the stairs by the door to the left."

I sprint downstairs and almost trip. My body slams into the bathroom door so hard that the handle punches a hole into the shabby drywall behind it. I fly to the closest sink and let my nose drip. By now the lower half of my face and neck are covered in blood. So are my hands and the front of my shirt. The blood is clotting and thick and stops up the sink. I hunker over, resting my forehead on the faucet, letting my nose run without paying attention to the world around me. I wait like this forever until the sink has an inch of blood in the bottom. It slows and I tilt my head upward to see myself in the mirror. To my surprise, someone is behind me. It is the girl. Her face is white as snow. I stare, wondering why she is in the men's bathroom. Then, mortified, I glance around the bathroom and see that there are no urinals.

"I'm so sorry," I say as my blood makes the drip-drip noise of a leaky faucet. "I thought this was the men's room."

"No, hey, don't worry about it ... are you okay?" She walks up and puts her hand on my shoulder.

"Yeah, well no, well, I'll be fine."

"Did somebody hit you?" She grabs some paper towels and starts wiping off my face. "Here, sit down," she says, pulling over a small trash can.

"No, nobody hit me."

"Here, keep your head straight, like this. So what happened? Did you fall or something?" She gently holds the paper towel against my nose.

"I have this problem, I get bad nose bleeds every once and a while. It's embarrassing."

"Oh, stop, it's nothing to be embarrassed about. I used to work in a hospital and have seen a lot worse than this." My nose stops bleeding and she wipes away most of the blood. I lean my head forward and rub my eyes.

"Headache?" she asks, putting her finger under my chin and lifting my head up. "Keep your head straight; you don't want it to start again."

She fishes around in her purse for a minute and pulls out a small bottle of pills. "Here, take two of these, they're Vicadin, leftovers from when I had my wisdom teeth pulled. They should help."

Grabbing the pills I look into her beautiful green eyes and smile.

"Why are you helping me? You don't even know me."

"Mona," she says, extending her free hand.

Hesitantly I shake it. "Dave."

"There, now we're acquainted. You and your friend aren't from around here. Everyone knows everyone in this shit-hole town and nobody knows you two. I like that."

"That explains the strange looks from people."

"Yeah, well people aren't receptive to foreigners around these parts." She zips up her purse.

"That still doesn't explain why you're helping me."

She smiles and looks away. "You really think I didn't notice you staring at me upstairs?"

"Staring at you until your boyfriend came in," I say, hiding my joy that she noticed me.

"He's not my boyfriend," she interrupts with resounding disgust. "It's complicated."

"It always is," I add.

We walk out of the women's restroom talking and laughing, quickly getting to know one another. The second the bathroom door shuts behind us I am hit with a star burst of light. When I open my eyes, I'm on the floor and my nose is bleeding again. A powerful hand grabs my shirt and lifts me off the ground. I'm eye to eye with the cop.

"Listen, you piece of shit!" He spits, sending small pieces of a fish fry into my face. "I don't know who you are or where you came from but nobody talks to my girl."

"I'm not your girl!"

"Shut the fuck up!" He points a finger in her face and she goes silent. "I'll deal with you later. Then he turns to me. "As for you, I want you out of my town by sun up. And so help me God, if I find you here tomorrow even a second after that sun comes up, I will kill you and nobody will ever know."

He lets go of me and I fall to the ground, scrambling on my hands and knees to get my back against a wall. He looks gigantic, almost grotesque in his police uniform; a mass of thick fatty muscles and unsightly bulges. "Pussy," he mutters, then turns his attention back to Mona. She shoots me a terrified look as he grabs her by the hair and drags her off. "I don't even want to know what the fuck you were thinking ..."

A woman comes out of the bathroom and tries to help me up. I push her hand away and sit on the floor, furious and ashamed, letting my nose leak all over. After a while I get up on my own and find my way back to the bar. The bartender looks like he has something to say.

"What?" I ask, sounding initially disinterested.

"Hey kid, don't let that guy get you down. I was gonna warn you earlier but you didn't seem like you wanted to talk. He's had it out for her for quite some time now. They dated in high school when he was quarterback, you know. And on prom night he beat on her ..."

"Listen, pal," I interject angrily. "I don't give a shit what his story is or her story either for that matter. Can I just get another beer?"

"Sure kid, this one's on me." He slides a Guinness across the counter and walks to the other end of the bar leaving me in my misery.

Sitting alone, waiting for Nick, I think of all the things I should have said. I fantasize about punching that cop in the face, kicking his ass, and saving Mona, who would run off with me. But run off with me where? That's when reality sinks back in. We're leaving tomorrow and I'm dying. That's why none of that happened and that's why I'm sitting here alone. Nick comes into the bar looking defeated and takes the stool next to me.

"You changed your clothes," I say.

"I don't want to talk about it."

"Where's what's her face?"

"I said I don't want to talk about it." He orders a Corona and glances at my t-shirt. "Where's your girl?"

"Left with the cop," I say, staring into my beer.

"What happened to your shirt?"

"The cop punched me in the face. Said he wants us out of town by sun up."

"Oh."

We sip our beers in tandem and then start laughing.

"So what happened with you and Cindy?"

Nick shudders and then takes a long drink. He reaches for my cigarettes and takes one out.

"We went out to the car and things were going pretty good. I thought she was hot with her clothes on, you should have seen her naked. We pulled the car around to a dark spot in the parking lot and went at it. I was in the driver's seat with my pants around my ankles, and she was straddling me." He takes a long drag from the cigarette. "Then, as we're really getting into it, I hear this noise."

"Noise?"

"Yeah, a noise," he says, and then stares down at the bar.

"Well, what was it? Don't keep me in suspense."

"It sounded like a wet, diarrhea fart."

I don't say anything; it's all I can do to keep from bursting out laughing.

"So I hear this noise and instantly I'm wet. My thighs, my knees, I can feel it dripping off the steering wheel onto me. And then there's this weird smell."

"She shit on you?" I say, not able to contain my laughter.

"No, that's what I thought, but no," Nick says. "She hops off of me and into the passenger's seat. She's crying and has her face in her hands. I look down, and there is this white-orange goo everywhere."

By now I am laughing so hard I'm crying. Nick won't even look me in the eyes he is so sickened.

"Stop, I don't want to know anymore."

"Oh no, you wanted to know so bad, and now you have to listen," Nick says. "So she tells me she takes diet pills. They block fat receptors so she can keep her hourglass figure. But if she eats to much fatty food, her body can't digest it … she called it an uncontrollable fatty anal discharge."

He takes a final long drag from his cigarette and then smashes it out in the ashtray. Then he slams the rest of his beer and sets down the empty bottle. "What do you say we get some sleep and then get the fuck out of this town?" I chug the rest of my beer, throw down a tip, and put my hand on Nick's shoulder.

"This place is like the goddamned Twilight Zone," I say, waving goodbye to the bartender.

We start the short walk back to the hotel to get a good night's sleep, in silent mourning of our terrible night. I stop for a second and put my arm around him.

"We may have lost the battle my friend, but we will win the war."

"I know and there are plenty more towns and plenty more women in between us and wherever we're going."

"Yeah, it just sucks."

"What's that?" He says, taking out the keys to unlock the car.

"Mona, the chick at the bar, I really liked her."

As we cross the street a guttural scream shatters the still night. Startled, we both look at each other.

"Let's get the hell out of here. I can't even imagine what else could go wrong in this fucking town."

"Come on!" I shout. "We're drunk, and I still have a craving for some adventure." I head towards the distant grunting noises. "Who knows, maybe it's Sasquatch?"

"When did you become so adventurous?" Nick mutters as he follows me

We track the noises to the parking lot of a boarded up grocery store. A cop car is double-parked across two handicapped spots. The noises are coming from the ground next to it. I can see the cop from the bar on top of Mona. His pants are around his ankles, his police baton shoved in her mouth.

I can hear her muffled screams. She is writhing under his weight. Her pants are torn open and her shirt is ripped and pulled up to her neck. I grab Nick, yanking him out of sight into an alley.

"Hey, isn't that?" he asks.

"Yeah, we need to do something."

"No way. He's a cop. And besides how do you know this bitch isn't into this?"

"She's not, fuck man, he's raping her. We have to do something. Go out there and create a diversion."

"And what the hell do you expect me to do?"

"I don't know; act drunk, it should come easy." I shove him out into the street.

In the alley I squat behind a big pile of garbage. It gives me a perfect vantage point of Nick, the cop, and Mona. Nick stumbles out of the alley staggering from side to side. Upon hearing him, the cop stands, pulling his pants up as fast as he can. He walks toward Nick pointing his baton and shouting.

"Hey drunk! Unless you want an ass beating you better get the fuck out of here!"

Nick ignores the cop's threat and walks right over to him.

"He ... he ... hey you, sssstay outta my way …"

"Fucking drunk, get the fuck out of here before you meet my revolver," the cop yells, grabbing Nick by his shoulders and slamming him to the pavement. From the ground Nick gives the cop the middle finger.

"Fuck you pig!" He spits on the cop.

"That's it drunk!"

The officer slams the end of his baton down into Nick's stomach and then spins, smacking Mona across the face with it.

"Don't think I forgot about you bitch. You stay right fucking there."

He advances on Nick. I've seen the Rodney King video and know what happens next. If there is a moment to be had this one is mine. I pull a jagged, rusty pipe out of the garbage pile I'm hiding behind. Charging out of the alley I swing at the cop with all my strength. The pipe lands just below the back of his knees with a satisfying crunch immediately sending him to the ground. With momentum on my side, I swing the pipe again, slamming it into his stomach. The cop lets out an awful gasp, rolls to his side and stops moving. In a rage I throw the pipe back towards the alley and pull out Spyder's switch blade from my back pocket. Nick must think I am going to kill him because he screams for me to stop. Flicking the blade out I snatch his radio off his belt and lean close to his ear.

"There's no calling for backup scum bag."

I stick the blade into a slot slicing off the receiver and smash the rest of it against the hood of his squad car. Before he can get his bearings, I cuff his hands behind his back and un-holster his pistol. He looks at me, dazed. Moving behind

214

him I press the gun into the back of his neck and cock back the hammer.

"How does it feel Mr. Officer?"

"What?" He blinks rapidly, still reeling from the pain of the blow.

"How does it feel to be a victim?" I thunk the top of his head with the butt of his gun.

"Oh fuck ... please don't kill me, I've got a fucking family ... I don't want to die!"

"And what would your wife think if she knew you were out here raping this girl in the middle of a parking lot?" I yell. "Nothing to say? Thought so."

"Listen, you better let me up you little fuck, you think I don't remember you from the bar? You're going to be in a shit load of trouble when I get out of this!"

Yanking his hair, I lift his head and press the barrel of the gun into his cheek. A not so gentle reminder of who is in control.

"*If* you get out of this."

"Oh shit," he begins to sob.

"Oh shit, indeed." I look over at Nick. "Help me drag this piece of trash into the alley."

"Gladly."

I prop him against the dumpster and cut his police badge off of his uniform. "You don't deserve this." Then I slide his wallet out of his back pocket and take his driver's license. "I am keeping this too. And I swear to god, if I ever see you again. If she tells me you came after her or if you try and arrest us, fuck, if I see you at the fucking grocery store, I'll finish the job you piece of shit."

We heave his body into the dumpster and slam the plastic lid shut; we keep him alive, which is more than he deserves. I pound the butt of the gun on the metal sides before leaving.

I wipe the prints off his gun using my shirt and drop it down a sewer drain. I grab his baton from the road, wipe it off and throw it on the roof of the grocery store. Then I see Mona. She is sitting in the middle of the empty parking lot crying. I sprint to her, close up her shirt, and wrap my arms around her.

"Mona, are you okay?"

She buries her face in my chest crying and rocking.

"Thank you," she cries.

"He can't hurt you anymore." I kiss her on the forehead. It's salty, damp with sweat. Her body is shaking in my arms.

"Nobody's ever stopped him before,"

I brush strands of stringy hair out of her eyes.

"Listen, Mona, we have to go now."

Her body goes limp in my arms as she drifts into shock. Her eyes are puffy and red. Her voice is scratchy from screaming for help. Her clothes are torn. And she now she is passing out. The shock of all the crimes we have just committed hits Nick. I hear him panicking while Mona wakes up and stares at the alley where we dumped the cop.

"Dave, we got to get the fuck out of here!" Nick pulls hard on the collar of my shirt.

"Mona, it was lovely meeting you, but we're leaving now." I stand up and she is still clutching my hand. Jerking my hand out of her grasp, I walk away with Nick, a lump forming in my throat.

"You're in love with her, aren't you?" he says, without even looking at me.

"Of course I am. Did you see what I just did to that cop?"

"I guess the feeling's mutual."

Mona is running down the middle of the street, her ripped denim jacket around her shoulders and her purse dragging at her side.

"Wait, Dave, wait for me … please wait, I'm coming with you!" she shouts, slamming into me with such force that she almost knocks me over.

"Mona, you can't come where we're going."

"I don't think you understand," she interrupts. "I'm coming with you guys. When he wakes up he'll find me. Do you have any idea what will happen? He's got friends, he can make me disappear!"

She stands in silence for a moment.

"Please," she pleads. "Take me back to my apartment so I can get my clothes."

I open my mouth to object but she puts her index finger over my lips.

"Shh …"

Stepping up on her tip toes she gives me a soft kiss on the lips. I'm not sure how much time I lost in that kiss but Nick pulls up in the car and rolls the window down, breaking our moment.

"Hey, love birds, lest you forget, we're criminals in this state."

Without saying anything she climbs into the back seat with me. Leaning forward over the center console she gives Nick directions.

"I live up the street. Go two traffic lights and make a right onto Clover Street. It's a brick building at the end of the street."

"Got it little lady."

I unconsciously roll over and put my arm around Mona to pull her close. My eyes open and my heart sinks deep in my chest as I realize I'm hugging a pillow, and not her. Sitting up in bed I scan the room. Her clothes and purse are gone, so are the car keys. This can't be happening. I fly out of bed, grab my pants and shirt in one handful and try to put them on as I move toward the door. I get to the door with no shoes on, my pants around my ankles and an arm through the head hole of my shirt. The electronic lock clicks and the door opens.

"Need a hand?" Mona laughs, juggling Styrofoam coffee cups and a bag of Dunkin Donuts.

"Mona, I wasn't expecting you …"

"Who else would it be?"

"That's not what I meant."

"What? Wait a minute …"She sets down the bag of food on the dresser by the television. "Did you think I took your car and left?"

I pause for a minute to carefully choose my words. "No, come here," I say, pulling my pants up. We sit at the foot of the bed and I pull my t-shirt off and put it on right. She doesn't say a word. The expression on her face says everything. "I'm sorry. It's just that my life up until this point hasn't left me the most trusting person in the world."

"You thought I left you? And took your car and everything? After what we went through just two days ago?"

"Well ... yeah. I did."

She turns toward me, pulling my head to her chest. "You poor thing."

"What?" I ask, my words muffled by her breasts.

Our heartfelt moment is interrupted by a banging on the hotel door. The banging is less of a request to enter more than it is an announcement of arrival. Nick walks in, drinking a beer, and sits down on the bed next to us.

"So what's the plan?" He chucks his empty bottle into a small trashcan with a clang.

"Good idea," Mona says, letting go of my ears. "We definitely need to have a discussion."

"Oh, Dunkin Donuts." Nick walks to the dresser and helps himself to the food and coffee.

"A discussion about what?" I lean over the bed to put my shoes on.

"Where are you two going?" Mona asks, bringing me an unsliced everything bagel.

"Nowhere," I say, taking the bagel and biting into it.

"Well, what's the plan?" she asks, sounding more confused. Unfortunately for her there will be no end to the confusion. Every answer will lead to more questions.

"We don't have one," Nick and I say almost in unison. Mona turns to the window and slides open the cheap beige curtain to reveal the drab view of the parking lot.

"You two have to be going somewhere. Who are you?"

I toss my half-eaten bagel onto the bed, walk up behind her, and put my hands on her shoulders.

"This is why I said you couldn't come. We have no destination, no plan. We're nobody important. Two guys seeing America on our own time. I'm a ghost walking along the backdrop of society and this is my guide," I point to Nick and he smiles.

"We're like Dante and Virgil," he laughs.

"But what about work? You two don't have jobs, right? How could you possibly afford this?" She turns around but keeps my hands on her shoulders.

"Just think of us as independently wealthy—"

"Not good enough." She jerks from my grasp. "I'm through running with criminals. Darin ruined my life, he cost me my nursing license … No I'm not going through this again."

"Darin?"

"The cop."

"Look Mona, we're not criminals. I inherited some money and this is my best friend. We just want to see the country, get a glimpse of the American dream before we return to our station in life," I explain. "We're not killers or drug runners; just two guys who have money they're not used to having. Trying to blow it and have a good time. So if you want to leave, this is our life not yours, I won't hold it against you."

She walks back and puts her finger under my chin, lifting my head a little. "Now was that so hard?"

Before I can answer she kisses me on the lips. We keep kissing for a few seconds until Nick clears his throat and I pull away from her.

"Was what so hard?"

"Telling the truth," she giggles.

She takes my hand and leads me to the bed, sitting me down between her and Nick.

"I was in when you saved me," she says. "And you did save me. But we should at least have a battle plan. Is there anything in particular you two would like to see? Anywhere you want to go?"

"Everywhere, and everything in between," I say without hesitation.

"Where have you been so far?"

"We went to New York City and stayed at the Chelsea. Tried to go to CBGB's but it was closed."

"A giant duck, we stopped and saw a giant duck," Nick throws in.

"We have pictures of us at every national monument in New York, but we don't actually remember them."

"You don't remember them?"

"No, we hooked up with this guy from some Australian band, The Deer Hearts. It was a whirlwind of drugs and alcohol. When we finally landed there were three days' worth of memories missing." I can sense Nick's disgust with how we acted in New-York; he won't even look at me while I tell our tale.

"What's the point of going places if you're too obliterated to remember you were there?"

There is a long hesitation between responses here. I've spent many restless nights since New York wondering what we did. Why we did it. If we're ever going to be caught for what we did at the Chelsea. But you can't move forward regretting the past. There is no going back, ever. You can only learn from your mistakes and try not to repeat them. And late at night when I am racked with guilt because I don't remember the view from the Empire State Building, I chalk it up to having a full rock star experience.

"We haven't been this way, it just happened. And by the time we realized it was happening, it was too late to stop."

"So where exactly are you going now?" She folds her arms, tapping her index finger against her elbow.

"Mount Rushmore," we say together.

"Well, that sounds exciting," she giggles, and then begins packing up her clothes. "When do you two want to leave?"

Seven hours later we are in the parking lot of Mount Rushmore. The drive was beautiful. Long winding roads lined with conifers stretching all the way to the clouds. We pay to get in, which bothers me slightly. This seems like one of those things you would want to show off for free. After parking we walk to the entrance, a small stone staircase with grey stone pillars. Looking right through them you can see the faces of our forefathers in the distance.

"Picture time," the tourist in me shouts.

Mona snaps a picture of me and Nick in the entryway just below the monument and then Nick snaps a picture of Mona and I kissing beneath it. We continue our climb in relative silence. Just being here is awe inspiring. Everything I wanted to feel in New York that was stolen by the drugs.

Later on, we pick out souvenirs in the gift shop. I bring a black hoody with a picture of the monument on it to the register and Nick picks out a ball cap. Mona comes out of an aisle with key chains hanging from her fingertips, postcards, t-shirts, and snow globes fill her arms. She drops the pile onto the countertop and requests a big bag.

"What the hell is all of this shit?" I ask before snatching my credit card away from the cashier.

"Would you trust me if I told you it's a surprise?"

"Fine."

Reluctantly I give my credit card back to the clerk and then carry the heavy bag to the car for Mona.

After leaving Mount Rushmore we gain momentum, no roadside attraction is off of the table. The world's biggest ball of yarn? We were there. The great Corn Palace of South Dakota, we went there too. Everyday something new, not holding anything back. I've never felt this alive and free. And all the while our car fills with junk. I bought Mona a separate suitcase just for the tourist crap she collects. Piles of postcards, snow globes, t-shirts, pictures, and key chains. And then I notice her staying up later, getting up earlier. She bought a small book light for the backseat, constantly doing stuff in the car.

"What are you doing?" I finally ask; it's three in the morning and we're in our tenth hotel.

"I thought you were sleeping." She pulls a piece of poster paper to cover the workstation she has setup at the room's desk. "I'm making an album of our journey, but I don't want you seeing it yet." She kisses me and I go back to bed.

We follow signs that read *"Where the hell is Wall Drug?"* all the way to a four story pharmacy in the middle of nowhere. We have lunch there next to a statue of a Jack-alope. A few days later we spend hours at the San Luis UFO Watchtower but aren't abducted or anal-probed. We have our pictures taken with some old whores at the Oasis Bordello Museum and drive to Blackfoot, Idaho, the potato capital of the world. I'm not sure why anyone would go to the potato capital of the world but we did. And we had a great time. Days turn to weeks, and then to months, as we lose track of our voyage from state to state.

Late one night, Mona's hard at work on her scrapbook.

"Well, can you at least talk to me about it while you work?" I can almost hear her smile as I say those words. "I'm having a hard time sleeping without you next to me."

"Sure babe. I'm pasting our pictures next to postcards and taping in the smaller souvenirs next to them. I've cut the logos off some of the t-shirts for page headers. I've always wanted to scrapbook at this level," she says, cutting out a picture of us and pasting it above a bumper sticker. "Now stop peeking and go back to bed."

Eventually, like road signs, the tourist traps begin to blend together. You've seen one crappy plastic souvenir you've seen them all. And then they're not enough. We begin stopping at town carnivals, flea markets, garage sales. We stop at a garage sale somewhere in Nebraska and buy a tea kettle for five hundred dollars, even though the price tag says fifty cents. The woman flips out when we tell her to keep the change. We scurry back to our car, joking about the world's most expensive teapot, while she tries to give the money back. Then we head to Four Corners Monument where the borders of Arizona, Utah, New Mexico, and Colorado meet.

"Ugh, how long can we stand in four different states?" Mona stomps her feet a little and puts her hands on her hips.

"Alright, switch, and let's make a circle of hands."

My companions start to show signs of exhaustion as we each rotate to the left. It took us almost 16 hours of driving to get here, counting bathroom breaks and dinners.

"When are we going to do something cool?" she says.

Mona has all of the mannerisms of a five-year-old not getting her way. Granted we have been doing more driving than seeing. Tension was bound to occur.

"I wish there was someone to take a picture of us," I muse out loud.

"Dude, we can wait here all year, nobody is going to come to this. It's hardly an attraction. I mean who really gives a fuck about standing in four separate states at the same time?"

"Fine, we can go, party poopers. But no more screwing around, we need a vacation from our vacation."

I can see a gleam in Mona's eyes as if she already knows what I am going to say. She lets go of our hands and throws her arms around my neck bringing her nose an inch from mine.

"And where are you thinking, baby?"

"Viva Las Vegas."

 *13*

For the fifth night in a row I can't sleep. My nightmares of Katrina are back from out of nowhere. Wicked dreams haunt me, reminding me that I'm wasting this poor girl's life. How could *we* ever have a future when I have no future? In my dreams Kat is a bloated putrefying corpse. Ripe with the stink of death, her flesh hangs off her body, exposing rotten veins and maggots. When I come into the hotel room she is telling Mona that I have brain cancer. And when Mona leaves, she leaps onto my back, sinking her yellow jagged teeth into my neck. I wake up with a headache and find myself down the hallway, refilling our ice bucket, just to have something to do. I go back in after a couple of cigarettes and Mona is wide awake, reading.

"Hey, babe," she says, laying her book face down on the bed. "Coming back to bed?"

I sit down on the bed next to her and drift into thought for a second. Drifting too far, I let the ice bucket fall to the floor and spill. "Are you okay?" She moves to clean up the ice. I stop her before she can stand.

"Mona, there is something I need to tell you before we go any further." I sit on the edge of the bed holding her hand.

"Yes?" Her voice is dreamy, telling me I am about to drop a mortar shell onto her perfect world. "Go ahead baby."

Letting out a heavy sigh I drop her hand and stand up. Tired, I pace at the foot of the bed and weave together a story I never thought I would have to tell.

"So that's it, I have a malignant brain tumor and I've opted out of treatment. This road trip is like my last hurrah."

She stays quiet, staring at the blanket, tracing the thread with her index finger. Then, as cool as can be, she stands without making any eye contact. Her slap makes a whip crack sound when it connects and stings like a freshly inked tattoo of her handprint on my cheek. But I don't stagger or flinch, I let her get it out. I know she is angry, hell, so was I.

"You asshole! How could you do this to me? And here my worst fear was that you would dump me a thousand miles away from home. Wait. Oh, that's right; I don't have a fucking home anymore!" She pauses to wipe the tears and smeared eye shadow from her face but it only smudges, making it worse. "I came with you and now you tell me this?"

"Mona," I grab for her hands but she yanks them away. "I'm sorry."

"Get out!"

"If that's what you want."

I step toward the door to go crash in Nick's room, but I turn around, only to see Nick standing in the doorway. I must have left the door open when I got ice.

"You've got fucking cancer?" he shouts in disbelief. "What?"

"Nick—"

I follow him across the hallway to his room. He stands in the doorway and scowls at me.

"You really are a selfish asshole," he says, slamming the door in my face.

The deadbolt locks on both rooms snap shut. I curl up on the scratchy carpet in the hallway and sob myself to sleep.

"Sir? Are you okay?"

A fat old hag is hunched over prodding at me with the rubber end of a metal cane. She jabs me between the ribs and then in my cheek.

"Ugh …" I groan, although the majority of my aches and pains are presently located in my heart. Rolling on my side I fish around the pocket of my jeans for some stray painkillers. The rest are locked in Mona's room. I find three and swallow them dry.

"Sir, there is a shelter down the street; if I catch you doing drugs in here again I am going to call the police."

"I not a homeless junky, I've got a fucking brain tumor and my girlfriend threw me out."

This woman either can't understand me or doesn't want to. I don't make any more fuss; I get up and walk to the gas station across the street to buy a pack of cigarettes.

Pacing the hotel parking lot it occurs to me that everyone has their breaking point. Maybe I've done it; maybe I've finally gone too far. Is it possible that they'll never unlock the doors to their rooms? What would become of me if I was abandoned? I have my wallet and credit cards so financially I'll be fine. But emotionally I'm not sure I could handle losing anyone else. My cigarette burns too close to the filter and I inhale a puff of plastic and gag. I flick the smoldering butt onto the sidewalk and walk into the hotel restaurant.

I'm alone in the restaurant, sadly nursing a plate of cold scrambled eggs and a cup of black coffee. From my booth I can see through the order window in the kitchen. The cook is an elderly woman with dingy white hair, straw-like stalks pinned in a bun. If I had to guess I'd say she was the owner. I try not to make eye contact as she sizes me up. Staring, trying to figure out why I'm sad. There is a motherly quality about her; she keeps sending the waitress to check on me. I tell her I'm fine for the thousandth time and fork an overdone home fry into my mouth. It's hard to be sad in public. In my experience people are generally good and want to help you, even if it's only to quell the negative vibes you're projecting into their space. I dunk a slice of toast sopping with butter into a pile of catsup and think back to how I got here. A lost soul, piloting a vehicle of other lost souls. That's what I've told myself, but is it true? It is starting to feel like whoever gets close to me gets sucked in to my darkness. Like at the center of the universe is me, shimmering dark, a black hole that devours everything good in life. Nick left it all behind for me; and look what I did to him. The lies. The reckless endangerment. What kind of friend does that?

Out of season Christmas bells hanging on the back of the diner's door clang against the glass as Mona walks in. The waitress greets her and points to my little corner booth. Mona comes over and sets her purse on the seat across from me. She slides into the booth scooting close to me.

"Hey."

I ignore her, moving food around, scraping my fork on the bottom of the porcelain plate.

"You know, if anyone should be mad right now it's probably me," she says, and I drop my fork to the table.

"What am I supposed to say here? Yeah, I lied to two people I care about. I fucked up and I don't know how to fix it this time."

"Stop." She puts her index finger over my lips. "I don't want you to do anything. I did a lot of thinking last night and I get it, it sucks, but it doesn't change anything. I still love you."

I put my head on her shoulder and she kisses me on top of my head. "But there's someone else who might need a bit more convincing."

"I know. I just don't know what to say. It's like when you tell one lie and then another lie to cover up that lie and then pretty soon your whole life is a lie—"

"I think you know what to say," she interrupts. "Start now, start at the beginning. Tell the truth. I talked to him; he's waiting for you in his room."

234

I don't deserve this chick.

Tossing down some cash on the table for the bill, I wave to the old woman in the kitchen, leaving Mona to order her own breakfast.

Back in the hotel I have to pound on Nick's door for 10 minutes before he answers.

"What the fuck do you want?" he shouts from inside.

"Room service," I say in a high pitched voice.

"Fuck you."

"Come on man, let me in, I think you know what I want." This time he doesn't answer and the volume of the TV rises through the metal door. "Just let me say what I've got to say!" I shout at the door. No answer.

Leaning my back against the door and sliding down to have a seat I put my head between my legs and rest my eyes. Before I know it the door gives out behind me and I fall half into his bedroom. The TV is off and Nick's trying to force me out the door. Grunting, I latch my fingers on to the adjacent bathroom door frame and pull myself in.

"You're finally ready to talk?" I say, standing up, and out of breath.

"No. It's been an hour and I couldn't see you out the peep hole. I thought you left."

"Well I didn't, and I want to talk."

"How convenient. Everything seems to revolve around what you want lately." He scowls in disgust.

235

"What can I do?" I ask, sitting down on the bed. "Please, I need you, anything. Let me make it up to you." I'm begging, pleading, and secretly praying.

"Fine. Start with the truth." He stands in front of me with his arms crossed, waiting.

This is it. The moment I've feared for a long time. Admitting the truth to someone else. Admitting it to myself. My eyes burn from a lack of sleep. Staring at the carpet I slowly raise my gaze to meet Nick's. I lean across the bed, pick up a bottle of rum from his nightstand, and pull out the cork. As quickly as I lift it to my lips he snatches it from my hands. He corks it and sets it on the dresser.

"No, you're going to do this clean and clear-headed."

I nod in agreement. Then, I let go, and feel a moment of release. My mouth breaks open like a dam and a flood of the truth comes crashing down. I start at the beginning, telling him about the day I was diagnosed, Katrina, Sally, group therapy. I tell him everything. When I come to the end of my story I'm drained and ready for a nap; it's both exhausting and relieving to finally have this burden off of me. Nick paces the hotel room like a caged animal. Then he stops and for the first time, he interrupts me.

"Well then why did she kill herself?"

"I told her I wasn't getting treatment. That I would ride it out until I was close to the end and let a bullet do the curing. Better than wasting away in a hospital."

"And she believed you?"

"I was serious. I had even bought a gun. By the time I had changed my mind it was too late. Survivor's guilt extremis. The day before she did it I bought an engagement ring, I was going to schedule an appointment …"

At this point I can't go on. Tears run down my face. My soul hurts. Nick sits down next to me and puts his arm around me.

"It's alright, you couldn't have known."

"No, it's not Nick, I did that to her. Just like I did this to you."

"Did what to me? Paid for me to go gallivanting across the country with you? You bastard." His sarcasm makes me chuckle through my tears. "It just hurt, you could have told me. I was always there and still am."

"I'm sorry," I say. Nick grabs me and gives me a tight hug.

"I know you are."

He lets me go and I sniffle, snorting up a bunch of snot. "So where do you want to go from here?"

"I thought you made that clear. We're going to Vegas." He smiles.

15

We're surrounded by a rainbow of high dollar luxury vehicles. Lamborghinis. Limousines. Hummers. Corvettes. Driving down the Vegas strip is cooler than driving anywhere else in the country. Unless, you're in our car, full of junk and clothes and food, and up to our ears in luggage. Then you're just as out of place as everywhere else. Nick drives around to the entrance of Caesars Palace. We have the top up to trap in the air-conditioning. As soon as we open our car doors the cool air disappears. It's so hot my sweat evaporates before it leaves my pores. Nick and I help the bellhops unload and then I give him a platinum credit card that I was approved for.

"Max this bitch out."

"Are you serious?"

"Yeah, fuck it. I'm going to die anyways. If they give you trouble just do cash advances and spend that. Oh, and I want that thing maxed by the time we leave."

"I would thank you, but that doesn't even begin to describe how I feel. I'll make you proud." He is delicate in taking the card, almost as if he fears it. He leans in close to my ear, "You sure about this?" He's not talking about the credit card.

"Yeah, never more sure about anything in my life."

"Well, good luck then brother."

I thank him and we hug, preparing to part ways for a while; it's a vacation from each other to cool the tension.

Inside our luxury suite, Mona and I spend the afternoon in the Jacuzzi ordering room service. Eating, napping, and soaking high above the city. Removed from the world. Letting every ounce of muscle tension be popped by the hundreds of bubble jets under water. At around six, we wake up and I tell her to go changed for dinner.

"Seriously? We've been eating for hours." She grabs her small pot belly and shakes it.

"We're on vacation in Vegas," I say. "I want to go out."

"Alright," she says, retreating to the bathroom. Inside is a beautiful strapless red dress that flares at the bottom. I bought it from the casino's gift shop and had it delivered while we were napping. She opens the door. "What's this?"

"Don't you want to have a nice night on the town?" I smirk.

An hour later I'm wearing a rented suit walking her out the entrance to our awaiting limousine. As the driver opens the door, she gives me that look as if to ask, *how did you plan all of this?* Our driver knows to take us on a tour of the entire city, casino by casino, until the sun goes down. He also knows that this trip ends at the Stratosphere.

"I hate heights," I say, my face smushed into the corner of the elevator, the only spot that's not glass. I grip Mona's hand so tight it's turning purple.

"You can see the entire city from here," she says, beaming with pure excitement. "It's so bright."

"I hate heights," I solemnly reiterate.

"Then why are we going up this?"

"Because there is something I have to do at the top."

"What?"

"You'll see."

We remain quiet while the elevator continues rising, thousands of feet above the sparkling city of Las Vegas. The doors of the elevator open to the inside of the Stratosphere. The entire restaurant exudes refined elegance as it rotates high above the strip, its glass walls providing an aerial view of the city. Ignoring the sheer awe of the restaurant itself, I pull Mona to the observation deck. This is where the world meets the universe. A dark sky hovers above the glowing monstrosity of a city. Illuminated with a billion neon lights, the city below seems to be looking at God and giving him the finger. Mona's grip now turns my hand purple.

"What is that?" she asks, with little tone or inflection in her voice.

"You said you liked rides."

"And you said you hated them."

"That's why I have to do this before I die. The Big Shot. You're blasted with 4G's on the upshot and then, right before it drops, there are five seconds of total weightlessness. And there's no line," I say, staring upward.

"Isn't that like four times the force of gravity?"

"Yeah," I say, trailing off in awe.

"I don't know. This is a bit much, even for me."

My arm tugs as she takes a step backward. I lift my free hand to her cheek and turn her gaze to mine. "Trust me," I say, planting a kiss on her lips.

We walk to where the line would form and pay for tickets. I help Mona into the seat and the attendant buckles us and checks our harnesses twice. My insides are so twisted it feels like I could shit puke. She latches onto my hand and I pull it free.

"You can't ... I mean, I'm sorry I can't hold your hand."

Before she can object the ride surges, propelling us into the sky. Her arms go rigid at her side. She seems more afraid than me and I know she's pissed that I won't hold her hand.

The chain clacks, and there is a loud blast as the hydraulic break pumps. We jerk and bounce in our seats, rocketing higher. I have to get this right because the ride is going to be over in less than 40 seconds.

One final clack and the chain releases us. My body is forced back into the seat as we soar toward the highest point of the Stratosphere. The force of the drop wrenches and pounds against my organs. The brakes screech, stopping us briefly, and then we jerk upward, firing up the next incline towards zero gravity. Fighting my body's natural response to vomit, I struggle to get the engagement ring out of my pocket. At the same instant I get the ring out we crest the top of the ride and I'm jerked forward. Then no pressure. In one second the ring jerks from my hand, shoots upward and stops in between our faces, at the precise moment of zero gravity. It hovers and floats between us, rotating in mid air. Mona looks at me.

"Will you marry me?" I scream at the top of my lungs, giving her only four seconds to answer.

"Yes!" she screams, and tries to grab the ring out of the air as we are yanked backwards.

Before she can grab it the ring sails upwards into the night and we begin our journey in reverse back to the start. I knew this would happen. The ring that sailed into oblivion was the ring I would have given to Kat. I have to let it go, just as I have to let her go. My sweaty hand is tight around the second box that holds a ring I picked out for Mona.

We stagger off of the ride together like a couple of drunks. My stomach is inside out but I'm not sure if it is from the exhilaration of the ride or hearing her shout yes. She stops, bends over and puts her hands on her knees. Just when I think she is going to vomit she stands up and leaps into my arms. Before I can brace for the impact, she slams into me and we're kissing in front of a growing crowd.

She pulls away from our kiss and stares at me with a wide smile, her skin glowing. "But the ring, it's gone," she says with a hint of childlike innocence in her voice.

Without any hesitation I drop to one knee and open the small case. She wipes tears from her eyes with a handkerchief she pulled from my suit pocket. She continues to nod without speaking as I stand and place the ring on her finger. The people who have gathered in a small circle around us are clapping. We lock arms and I lead her through the restaurant to a reserved table where roses and champagne await us.

Seated, she places her napkin across her lap and takes a sip of merlot. She gazes at me with a kind of half-awake dreaminess in her eyes. But the dreaminess holds an element of intensity; as though her eyes see straight into my soul.

"What's wrong?" I say, instinctively knowing that she is deeply contemplating something.

"What could possibly be wrong? This is perfect, this whole night."

"Well then what's on your mind?"

244

There is a pause, one of the most uncomfortable ones I have lived through. An eternal moment of retrospection that lasts longer than a single sip of wine. Longer than two. Long enough for the waiter to come and take our order. Long enough for her to finish and order another glass of merlot. I use this time to look out the floor to ceiling glass windows, enjoying the collage of night city lights.

"I imagine we'll be married before morning," she says, tracing her finger around the bread plate. "Being that we're in the marriage capital of the world." Then another pause, not as long as the last, but long enough for me to break.

"Well, unless you want to wait, but time isn't really on my side," I say.

"No, no, you've been a dream come true since we met. But if we do this I am going to need something from you."

Here it comes. Access to the money, a life insurance policy, this is when the bleeding begins. But this time it's not my nose it's my heart. And things were going so well. She won't even look me in the eyes right now. And then she does, and she reaches across the table and takes my hand.

"I need the truth from this point forward," she says. "You've told some pretty grievous lies, and that needs to stop."

This statement hits me hard. For so long it was hard for me to trust anyone. Let alone love them. How can I trust anyone when I can't even trust myself? And the same goes for love. I don't love myself. If I did I wouldn't treat my body like a dumpster, polluting it with truckloads of drugs and alcohol. If I loved my body I would go to a doctor, get the help I need. But this isn't about me, it's about her. Mona and her beautiful smile, her genuine spirit. Her innocence. I always thought it was Kat, but I guess I really didn't trust her either. She couldn't handle "us." And proof of that was her suicide. She left me here to deal with this world of shit on my own, and I'm starting to think that's okay. I'm starting to believe that her death was meant to happen, because it brought Mona and me together.

This is where things change for me. Right at this table, under the scent of roses and red wine. This is where I realize that there is no doubt in my trust and love for this woman. Everything that comes out of her mouth is straight from her heart. There is no money. No greed. No hidden desires or ulterior motives.

She knows me.

She knows my secret.

And she is still by my side. Following me God knows where.

"I'll do anything for you. I love you."

After dinner, our limo takes us to Las Vegas' only drive-through wedding ceremony. Nick knew to meet us there; I made sure of this because I at least want my best friend present when we get married. When we arrive he's waiting in a rented tux next to a big pink Cadillac.

"So it went well?" he says, helping Mona into the backseat.

"Did you really think I would say no?" she laughs, kissing me on the cheek. Nick takes the spot in the driver's seat; it seems a fitting duty for the best man to drive us through.

He navigates us along the Tunnel of Love Drive-Thru. The roof of the tunnel is painted like a sky, blue at the edges and dark towards the center, with elegantly painted stars, half-moons, and cherubs. It's not the marriage I had pictured when I was a kid, but it's appropriate. An Elvis impersonator at the window performs the ceremony. In less than a minute, it's over. Once we sign our names in the right spots, two become one. Nick pulls the Caddy out the other end. He hugs and congratulates us both.

"I never thought I would see this day," he laughs and takes a sip from his flask.

"Thanks for being part of this," I say, hugging him again.

"I wouldn't have missed it for the world. But now you two kids need to go enjoy your honeymoon and I need to get back to this," he holds up the American Express card I gave him.

We say our goodbyes to Nick and return to the limo. In our luxury suite at Caesars Palace, we begin a proper honeymoon. I carry Mona over the threshold. Inside a gigantic plate of chocolate covered strawberries and a bottle of champagne sit on the table. A path of fresh rose petals leads to the bed. We head straight to the hot tub, leaving a trail of clothes in our wake. We feed each other strawberries and get drunk on expensive champagne.

"You know, I've always wanted to see the Great Salt Lake," she says, sipping her tall glass of champagne.

"Then that is where we go after our honeymoon and vacation is over."

"Deal." She raises her glass and clinks it against mine.

17

After a few weeks of honeymooning, Las Vegas starts to lose its appeal. An excess of gambling, gourmet food, and shows has us itching for some real adventure. One can only watch the Blue Man Group and David Copperfield so many times. I rent and pick up a town car before Mona wakes for the day. She's become a late sleeper and that gives me time to get everything we need for the day. I pack three meals and a case of bottled water into a cooler because of the heat warnings I read in the brochure. I also grab our camera. Most importantly, I remove Katrina's box from our suite and place it in the trunk. It's time I make good on a promise I made over our engagement dinner. Thankfully Mona had not noticed it among my luggage in the room. She saunters into the living room with sleep still in her eyes and I flick off the TV.

"Ready to go?" I say, standing with keys in hand.

"Go where?" she asks, rubbing her eyes. "Back to bed?"

"No, I was thinking of a picnic." I jangle the car keys in front of her face. "Everything is ready to go except you."

"Alright, 10 minutes."

249

Forty minutes later we're traveling along the Great Basin Highway outside of the city. We're met with a great nothingness for quite awhile; only dust and rock until we make our turn onto the Valley of Fire Highway. Then more nothing, save for the occasional roadside campground. This road leads us straight into the Valley of Fire State Park. One $10 admission fee later, we're unloading the car in the most shaded place we can find.

"I can feel myself melting," Mona whines as I set down the cooler in the shade.

"We've got ice, water, and plenty of food. What more could we ask for?"

"Air conditioning."

"Don't be that way. Would I have brought you out here for no reason?" I unload the final parcel from the trunk and set it next to the cooler. This tattered cardboard box has survived quite a journey to end up here.

Mona slumps into one of the folding lawn chairs, closes her eyes and fans herself with the Valley Brochure. Sitting Indian style on the desert ground I take a deep breath and peel the tape off the cardboard box. It has lost all of its stickiness and crunches when I fold it back. Piece by piece, I unpack it. Like a Shaman about to lead a vision quest, I take the items out in order. First I unfold the green and white flannel blanket we used at our rooftop picnic. I lay it out. Next, I pull out a hot pink photo album with a small silver plate engraved on the

250

front cover. The etching reads *For David*. Then the wristband from the night I picked her up at the hospital, I can't believe she saved it. A small heart shaped box of chocolates I gave to her at Le Mousseu's on Valentine's Day. The chocolates are gone, but inside are ticket stubs from the places we went together. Movie stubs, amusement park tickets, dinner receipts, everything. She saved everything. The last thing I pull out is what I put in, her suicide letter. Seeing my name in her elegant script on the front produces a lump in my throat. Fighting the tears I place the letter on the blanket next to everything else.

"Baby, come here."

She opens her eyes and is no longer concerned with overheating. Kneeling next to me on the blanket she drops the brochure and studies everything. Mona has a gentle, reserved quality about the way she examines the objects, as if she is exploring artifacts in a museum. She traces her fingers around the edge of the photo album. Places her index finger just under my name on the envelope. Tilts the heart shaped box open just enough to peer inside. But never once does she pick anything up.

"What is this?" she asks wide-eyed.

"I've never seen what's in this box. The most I did was slide that opened letter in and seal it back up. I …"Tears force their way out and down the side of my face. I close my eyes for a minute, not making a sound, and then open them to look at Mona. "This is the past, my past. We've grown together, shared in each other's lives, and now it's time I share mine. This is part of the reason I had to leave home."

I wipe the tears from my cheeks. "I told you no more lies or secrets, and this might be my biggest one."

Mona doesn't say a word. She glides her right hand across the objects as if some type of energy is emanating from them. It takes her a few minutes to do anything more than this. Her hand hovers over the wristband for longer than anything else. She raises it up to her eyes squinting at the label.

"Who is Katrina?" she asks without the slightest hint of anger.

"Katrina is the woman I loved before you. This is the box she left to me. And the envelope with my name on it contains her suicide letter."

There is a distinct pause in Mona's gentle nature. The missing emotion is somewhere between bewilderment and curiosity. She sets the wristband on the blanket in its original spot.

"I'm so sorry," she says, reaching out and taking my hand. "Why did she do it?"

"I don't know for sure. All I have are ideas and nightmares. I've never read the letter, or gone through the box. That's what I want you to do ..."

"I can't do this," she interrupts. "She left these things for you; it was her wish that you would get them and maybe understand. I can't."

"That's fine. I prepared for this and I totally understand. But I'll go to my grave before I read that letter. This is the most personal thing I have ever shared with anyone. I haven't even shared it with myself." I begin to pick up the items and put them back in the box. Mona jerks me back to a seated position on the blanket.

"Stop." She squeezes my hand. "I can do this for you."

Deep down I knew she would.

"Thanks. I'm going to have a walk. I'll be back later."

I give her a quick peck on the lips and leave her with Kat's box. I'm not sure what she'll do when I return, but this had to be done, the truth will set me free.

I walk around the desert, giving her enough time to read the letter and look through the album. Thirty minutes of hot and dry. She made me bring a bottle of water when I left and in a half an hour I drank it all. On the way back my mind drifts to my own demise. I wonder if this is what hell will be like. Endless miles of boiling hot dry rock stretched before you and nothing but an empty water bottle. I deserve no less for all of my lies.

Tired, I find a large rust-colored rock formation and sit cross-legged beneath its shade. Despite the raging heat, it's meditative being alone out here. In the distant heat waves, I see a body materializing. Mona comes towards me with a white towel wrapped around her dark black hair. She's wearing mirrored aviator sunglasses and a bright white dollop of sun tan lotion on her nose. Without a word she sits next to me and takes my hand. She slides a water bottle out from inside her pink backpack and presses it against my forehead.

"I told you that wouldn't be enough water," she smiles, sniffling a little. "It's not your fault …"

"Stop, I told you I don't want to know." I let go of her hand, twist off the cap of my water bottle and take a long drink.

"No, Dave, this is where you listen."

"Stop!"

"No, she loved you, more than her own life, and you need to understand that." Mona puts her hand on my cheek, moving my face to meet hers. "That letter was the most powerful thing I've ever read. It told a story, along with the photo album, of a love built from tragedy. She couldn't live without you, Dave, it wasn't your fault."

"But I wasn't going to kill myself," I blurt out, my tears evaporating into the desert heat. "This wasn't how it was supposed to happen."

"Yes, it was, because it did. And what if things hadn't happened this way? What if you and Nick never wandered through the parking lot? How many more times would Darin have raped me? Used me up before throwing me away? Everything happens for a reason."

254

I lean my head against the rock. She's right. This has all unfolded exactly how it should have. Because that's the only way it could have.

"You need to promise me something," she says, taking my hand again, waiting for acknowledgement.

"What?"

"You need to read that letter before you, you know. I want you to have the peace you deserve. There is no reason for you to carry this around any longer." She slides the letter out of her backpack and places it in my hand, closing my fingers around it. "Please baby, for me."

"Okay." I fold the letter in half, sliding it into my back pocket. "I will, but only when I'm ready."

She smiles without saying anything and kisses my lips. The sun is now off in the distance, getting ready to set. I stand on wobbly legs, extend my hand and pull Mona to her feet.

"What now?" she says, as we hike back to the campsite.

"Air conditioning and a pool, then Nick and the open road."

"Good, Vegas is getting stale," she laughs.

Because of today, I decided to keep Katrina's letter in my back pocket from now on. Not only to honor my promise to Mona, but because maybe she's right, this burden is heavy and I'm very tired.

18

Everything was going good until we hit Utah. My nightmares match my headaches in magnitude. I wake up with cold night sweats. I'm unable to sleep for days at a time and then I nod off in the car and wake up in strange places, places my companions swear I told them to take me. The disease is up and I'm down. It impairs my motor skills. Some days I wake up, talking like a stroke victim. After a week of this I decide it's time to put my affairs in order. I make phone calls, fax documents, all to ensure Nick and Mona are put on my accounts so they can access money after I die. If only to get back home and go back to their lives. Whatever lives they have left.

We find a small townie bar tonight when we get to Salt Lake City. Mounds of peanut shells crunch under our feet as we make our way across the unvarnished wood floor. There's not one flat screen TV in here, which is important. We want to keep it simple tonight, finalize our plans, and I want to get shitty in the process. Confronting my own mortality head-on has left me with little fear. The bar is sparse, with a few older men glued to their stools. Long term, professional drunks, nobody our age. This is good because it means we can get fucked up without explaining ourselves, without having to tell a story. I can be free to drink and drug to my hearts content The bar doesn't serve any food, although the bartender offered to order us a pizza. I politely decline. Alcohol and pills are the only fuel I will need for this death bash.

"A toast to the future, your future." I raise my glass.

Nick and Mona exchange uncomfortable glances before raising their glasses to toast my death. I take three Vicadin and a Lortab out of my pocket and wash them down with a shot of Patron. I've developed quite the tolerance.

"So it's settled then, you two know what to do?"

"We make arrangements to have you cremated, and then divide up what's left of the money and move on." Nick's voice is monotone, cracking when he says the word cremated. "Now can we try and have a good time tonight?"

"Who's not having a good time? I'm having a great time." I throw back another shot of Patron. "Let's fucking party!"

They look at each other, making no motion to join me in a death bash.

"Fine, I'm going outside to smoke, party poopers."

When I come back, one of the barstool heroes has his arm around Mona. She writhes and pushes it off, trying to order drinks while ignoring his onerous advances. But he

257

persists, his body language saying; *I'll take it, whatever I want.* He reminds me of the cop back in Iowa. He's a chubby bastard in a cheap black suit with a bulbous red nose blotchy with burst capillaries. He must always look like he's blushing. The only nice thing about him is the expensive leather jacket he has wadded up on the bar.

I scan the room for Nick, wondering what he's doing. Why would he let this happen? I spot him leaning on the pool table flirting with another bar slut. I fish the switchblade out of my back pocket.

Calm, calculated, and quiet, I approach from behind until I'm pressed tight against his back without him even noticing. Maybe it's all the pills I took, or that I mixed them with booze but I feel invincible right now. Seeing this pig with his arm around my wife pushes me over the edge. I bring my arm around his neck and flick the blade open with one fluid motion. Before he can react I'm pressing the dull side of the blade into one of his fat rolls over his jugular, just to give him a scare.

"Choose your next words carefully friend."

"Uh …"

"What? You didn't know she was taken? She is wearing both a wedding and engagement ring. Or maybe you just didn't care?"

"Listen buddy, I didn't mean anything by it, how about you put the blade down and we both walk away."

Pressed against his back, I can feel his body trembling against mine. I can also feel Mona's look of disgust. I click the blade shut and slide the knife into my jacket pocket. Slowly he steps away from me and backs out of the bar.

"You're such an asshole sometimes," she shouts over the jukebox. "He was fucking harmless, some old perv, I can handle myself." She leaves the drinks on the bar and storms outside before I can respond. I slam another tequila shot and wash down two Oxycontin before turning to chase her. Nick steps in front of me at the door.

"You need to take it down a few notches," Nick says, blocking me. "I don't know what your fucking deal is but chill the fuck out. You're out of control. Everybody in here saw you pull a knife on that guy. Do you want to get arrested?"

"You didn't know when to back off about Kat and you don't know when to back off now. So get the fuck out of my face before I return that black eye you gave me at my apartment."

I'm pointing my finger in his chest and spitting into his face. Drunk, high on pills. This disease eating away at my very core. Sad thing is he's right. This moment feels like a turning point, dulled by the exotic combination of alcohol and narcotics. He's right about how I've been. He's right about my drinking and self-medicating. That's what I call it, self-medicating. When in actuality it has developed into a full blown drug addiction. The cancer isn't making me do this and

Nick and Mona are just trying to stop me. There's no logical reason for this. But when I think of their words, their actions, it lights a fire in my belly. It infuriates me beyond words. On one hand I want to stay here, cool off, sober up, and go home. But that inexplicable burning rage tells me to chase after her. It urges me to pick a fight. Even though she's right. It urges me to argue with her until we fall asleep in separate rooms. Even though I just want to cuddle. Even though I just want to be back in control of my body. This internal conflict screams from within, until I can't even stand the sight of Nick.

So I push past him and stagger out the door.

"Mona!" I shout, bracing myself in the door frame as the world starts to spin. Losing my grip on the door I trip out onto the sidewalk and gimp to the entrance of an alley beside the bar. "Mona, come back!" Out from the darkness in the alley comes a fist landing square in my face. Thanks to the pills it doesn't hurt, but the blow still shorts out my brain circuitry sending me to the ground. When I regain consciousness my arms are being held behind my back and the pudgy guy from the bar is shouting at me and punching me in the face and stomach.

"Wake up, fuck!" He smacks me across the face. "You think you can come in here and push people around?"

I struggle while he winds up to hit me again. My arms are locked behind my back by someone much stronger.

"Do you know who I am?" He slams his fist into my stomach. "Do you know who you fucked with?" The man holding my arms back prevents me from falling as this asshole drives another punch into my stomach. It gurgles, reminding me of what I ate earlier. Luckily the pain killers have left me pretty numb. "Are you ready to talk you little puke?"

"I'll talk! I'll talk!" I shout, hoping to appease him.

"Well maybe I don't want to listen." He backhands me across the face, splitting my lip, sending blood to the asphalt. "Maybe I just want to hit!"

His knee comes up into my stomach and my body struggles to fall to the ground but his goon has a strong hold on me. He yanks on my hair, lifting my head up to his. He looks directly in my eyes. "I didn't even want to fuck your ugly wife," he says, smacking me across the face. My left canine loosens in my gums. "Okay, now I'm ready. Talk! Tell me something that will make me want to stop hitting you."

Bloody drool oozes down from my limp head, drawing a crimson line to the pavement. My lip is split in several places and there is a gash on my right cheek from the big gold ring he is wearing.

"If you want answers you need to ask the right questions," I say with hatred in my eyes. "You should be asking if I give a shit who you are!"

I spit a large glob of phlegm and blood into his face and he drives another punch across my jaw. His fist makes a

261

cracking sound and nearly half of my teeth rattle loose. My mouth tastes like dirty copper wire. My body is starting to hurt.

"Oh you little fucker." He wipes the glop of spit out of his eye. "You've got a fucking death wish don't you?"

"You don't even know the half of it," I growl, bringing my foot up into his crotch. At the same time I muster what strength I have left and smash the back of my head into the front of the goon's face. Warm blood drips down the back of my neck. He loses his grip and I fall to the ground. I sidestep these maniacs, trying to run around them and out of the alley, but something, a pipe or stick, slams into the back of my knees. I haven't felt much pain until now, this hurts. I fall to my knees, gashing my arm on a broken beer bottle. Then I feel a pair of handcuffs clasp shut around my wrists.

"I'll take it from here, boys," A familiar voice says from the dark. A man steps out and hands the pudgy guy a wad of cash.

"This little shit was hard to find." The pudgy bastard drives a kick into my ribs, the point of his boot rips through my shirt, cracking a rib. He leans down an inch from my face. "That's right cocksucker, we've been tailing you." He kicks me in the stomach again, this time so hard I puke onto the sidewalk. "Should have paid more attention."

"Enough. I'll take it from here." He stops the pudgy man from savaging me any further. "Help me get this piece of trash in the trunk. We're all going to go for a little ride."

The dark man leans down close so I can finally get a look at his face. My stomach cringes, it's Darin, the cop from Iowa. He places a black bag over my head and cinches it shut around my neck. And then I pass out.

19

The air is cold, damp and still, like fog, and the ground beneath me is hard and bumpy. The three men are standing far enough away from me that their voices are hushed. It smells like earth. The quiet talking stops and I hear footsteps approaching. A hand grips the top of the black bag and yanks it off, taking a bit of my hair with it.

I scan my surroundings. A car faces me, its high beams blinding me. I squint and can see Darin, the cop from Iowa, standing in front of me with the black bag in one hand and a gun in the other. Funny, I get the feeling he plans on killing me, and I've only ever heard his name once. There is a thick rope loosely around my neck, binding me to the tree I sit against. The two guys from the bar stand next to Darin.

"We meet again, friend," Darin says, squatting down to my level and rubbing the gun across my cheek. "How's that feel?"

"Are you going to kill me?"

"Maybe. Or maybe I just want to show you something." Darin spins around and puts a bullet in the leg

264

and chest of the pudgy guy. Before the second goon can react, Darin shoots him in the kneecap. The shots ring harshly in my ears.

"Oh, my God, my God… oh God…" The man on the ground screams, holding his leg. Darin walks over to him, pointing the gun down at his face.

"Why?" he pleads. Darin pulls the trigger and the bullet rips a hole through his skull.

Fuck. All over a girl. My stomach tightens after seeing the two men murdered. Darin comes back over to me and places an unlit cigarette between my lips.

"You're probably going to need this," he leans down to light it, a single comfort before I die. *Kat, I could really use a guardian angel right now.* Just as the flame is about to touch the tip of my cigarette he drops the lighter to the ground and smacks the cigarette out of my mouth. "Yeah right, you don't deserve it," he laughs

"Why are you doing this? Over a girl? What the fuck is wrong with you?" I shout.

"You think this is cause of that dumb bitch? Really? No!" He presses the cold gun barrel into the center of my forehead. "This is because I lost my job, my wife. This is because after I was found I couldn't explain anything, nobody believed my lies anymore." Sweat pours from his body. His hands shake, and the gun vibrates against my cheek. "I lost it all. This is for what you took, my house, my wife, my kids, and my position. This is for me. Ah! Fuck!" He turns away, pacing in front of the car between the two corpses, beating himself on the head with the butt of the gun.

He walks out of sight for a second and I hear the door of the car open and close. He returns, at a distance, with a gun in each gloved hand. The guns explode in my direction, a fury of bullets zipping around me. Every muscle in my body tightens and I squeeze my eyes shut. Deaf again, terrified, I wait for the painful strikes of the gunfire. When nothing happens I open my eyes. He shot up the tree I'm tied to and a few of the surrounding trees. Carefully, he places a gun in each of the corpse's hands. Then he retrieves his original revolver from a concealed shoulder holster. The same pistol I held to his head in Iowa.

"Have to make it look like a shootout," he says, fishing in his pocket to produce a handcuff key. He places it in my hand. "Free yourself, and be quick."

"Why should I?"

"Because this can't look like a murder," he explained. "The money I gave those scum bags to find you was stolen. Drug money that never made it into evidence. There are kilos of coke in the car. The last piece of this is you, running into the woods, bleeding to death from a fatal gunshot wound after the deal goes bad. And I return a hero."

"And what if I don't run?" I look at him with defiance, taking in this entire experience with all my senses. My red

266

flesh bulges around the cold wet metal of the handcuffs. Fresh dew in the high grass dampens my jeans. A starlit night sky above. A scratchy hemp rope dangles loose, itches the back of my neck. These could be my last earthly sensations before a bullet cures my brain cancer.

Darin squats down and leans in really close to my face. His breath fills my nostrils with the stink of sour whiskey. "I'll tie the other end of that fucking rope to the bumper of my car and drag you halfway across this state." His eyes are dark, his smile twisted, and his words ring with truth. Running while he shoots at me is the only chance I have.

Taking the handcuffs off is difficult even with the key. I drop it a few times, my nerves shot, but finally I unlock them. Letting them fall to the ground, I rub my wrists and stand up. Darin takes out a pocket knife and slices the rope at the tree.

"Leave it around your neck, just in case I need to drag your dead ass to re-stage the crime scene. Now run." He tilts his head forward ever so slightly and raises the gun. "Run that way!" He points the gun towards the car.

With my eyes adjusted to the light I can see that beyond the car is a grassy field stretching for at least a mile. To my right and behind me are woods, to my left is Darin. I sidestep the tree I was tied to, double back and head into the woods at full sprint. His gun pops and a bullet zips by me cracking into a nearby tree. This time I don't flinch. I fight every sore muscle in my body, clench my fists and run. Sticks and leaves crunch beneath me as I leap over dead logs, trying to put as much distance as I can between myself and my killer. He assails me with taunts as well as bullets. But I can tell by the echo of both his voice and the gun shots that I am getting further away. Losing my concentration, I trip over the rope still dangling from my neck and spill to the ground.

I can't do this anymore. This constant struggle to stay alive or die. Maybe I stop running from death and just wait. My adrenaline comes down and I realize there is something in my hand. I sit with my back against a pine tree and unclench my fist to find the mangled cigarette and lighter, I must have picked them up when I took the cuffs off. I slide the rope off my head and light the cigarette, inhaling deep for what could be the last time. Darin's taunts are growing louder. Twigs snap as he barrels through the forest like a tornado with a loaded gun. I wait with the patience of a monk, a devout student of death. He can see the cherry of my lit cigarette now. He comes around the Douglas fir and levels his gun at the tiny red burning light.

"Hope that smoke was worth it," he says, pulling the trigger.

As the bullet blasts out of the gun I step out from behind the pine tree, throw the rope around his neck and jerk him off of his feet, throwing the gun into a pile of leaves. He struggles, thrashing his head and limbs while I strangle him. His eyes are still locked on the red hot cherry of my cigarette, burning out, tucked in a branch. I place my knee in the center of his back and wrench the rope hard, bending his body into a u-shape. And then the rope snaps, sending me careening backwards onto my ass. Darin is limp, but that means nothing. I scramble around in the dark groping around for the gun. My hands grasp at dead leaves and sticks and mud. Nothing. He crawls on his hands and knees looking for the gun, too. Fuck it. I bolt back to the car. We weren't as far away as I thought. Sprinting out of the woods, losing strength, my head is pounding. I dive onto the chubby guy and grab the gun from his lifeless hand. Rack the slide and look inside, it's loaded.

"You should have killed me!" Darin screams, walking out of the woods, gun in hand. We raise our guns to each other. He smiles. "You don't know if that's loaded."

"I checked."

"You think you're a better shot than me?"

A bullet cracks, ripping through the right side of his chest. His body wrenches backwards, the revolver flies from his hand. It doesn't look at all like it does in the movies. I fall to my knees paralyzed by fear waiting, for what I don't know. He doesn't move. He doesn't try to uncoil his twisted arm and reach for the gun. He doesn't moan or cry. Nothing. It's right then I realize that those were his last words.

I crawl behind the car so I don't have to look at any of the bodies. I throw up. I cry.

I put an end to it. It had to end. This beast, a rapist who abused the power of the law. A monster, cheating on his wife, forsaking his position as husband and provider. A man who was willing to track, kidnap, and murder for revenge. How much further would he have chased us? I think of Mona.

The proof of my love lies in the blood and bodies surrounding me. If I had died, he might have found her. If I turned him in to the police, he would have waited to find her. I'll admit that I don't feel right. But suddenly, I don't feel quite as bad for killing him.

20

I left everything there. Who knows how long it will be before anyone finds any of it? The only things I grab are my cell phone and a pack of cigarettes from the glove compartment of his car. I follow tire tracks in the grass with little more than my thoughts. *I just killed a man.* My stomach cringes. It's a long walk until this dirt road turns into asphalt.

I think about Mona, and how I protected her. At the grocery store, at the bar, and finally, here. I love her so much. I think of Nick. I wonder what he'll do when I'm gone. What she'll do when I'm gone.

Then it occurs to me that I'll be gone sooner rather than later. I begin to cry again as I walk down this desolate road. For the first time, I really don't want to die. I want to get help, I want to get well. I want to take care of and protect Mona for as long as I can. Suddenly the time I have doesn't seem long enough. An eternity doesn't seem long enough.

And then I think of Katrina.

Am I doing the same thing to Mona that Katrina did to me? I replay events in my head. Try to see different outcomes. Try to imagine what life would be like if I got better. If I never went on this crazy trip. If I had proposed to Kat.

Then it hits me. *Mona's right.*

This played out exactly how it was supposed to, because it's the only way it could have. My phone chimes indicating I have service. It still takes another hour of walking before I find a cross road with street signs. I call Nick.

"Hey, where the hell have you been? We were worried sick."

"It's a long story. I'm at the corner of Creek and Munson roads. I'm not really sure where, it's pretty rural out here. I have no idea how to get back."

"Oh okay, so you get drunk and high on pills and wander off, and it's our job to come find you? Fuck that—"

"Nick, I just shot a guy."

Silence. He knows I won't lie to him anymore. It only takes a second for me to realize that I am sobbing loudly.

"What? Are you shitting me?" he yells into the phone.

"Just come and get me. Things got bad, very bad. I'm going to sit down in the bushes by these street signs. I don't want anyone to see me out here. Grab the GPS, plug in the cross roads, and please come find me. And don't bring Mona."

"Yeah … sure."

An hour and nearly half a pack of cigarettes later I see headlights coming down the road, slowing at my intersection. When it materializes out of the fog and I am sure it's our car, I step out into the road and climb in. Nick does a U-turn and we head home. We stay silent for almost 15 minutes while I chain smoke, lighting new cigarettes off the butts of my old ones. I'm sobbing, I can't look at him. I'm a murderer.

"Are you going to tell me what happened out there? Or don't you remember?"

"What's that supposed to mean?"

"Oh, I don't know, your drug habit? The alcoholism? Or maybe your cancer made you do it?"

"You're going to regret that."

"Whatever."

"The two guys at the bar."

Nick slams on the brakes and the car screeches to a halt. "The ones hitting on Mona? You fucking killed them? What the fuck man? Just because you have a fucking death sentence doesn't mean you can go around killing people!"

"I didn't kill them. They kidnapped me. Darin, Mona's ex, paid them to track us down. Lucky for you they only grabbed me."

Nick pulls the car back out onto the highway and resumes our course. "Holy shit. Are you serious, the cop?"

"I guess he lost his job when they found him. Took his badge, his wife left him and took the kids. And he snapped, came after us. Then he shot the two guys he paid to find us and chased me in the woods, hunting me." I begin to cry harder, dropping my cigarette into my lap and searing a hole in my

273

jeans. "I just wanted to get the hell out of there. It didn't have to be this way."

Nick puts his right hand on my shoulder offering some comfort. "It's alright; you did what you had to do."

"I killed him, Nick."

"I know, but you got away from him, and now it's over. We can call the cops and then never have to worry about him again."

"No authorities. We get out of here. He made that whole crime scene look like a drug deal gone bad. He shot guys with different guns, shot up the trees. Placed a ton of coke and money in the car. I cleaned my prints off of everything. We're close enough to the border that it could look like a cartel deal gone bad; at least that's what he said."

I pull down the mirror and look at my face. They really beat the shit out of me. My left eye is swollen shut, it's a miracle I was able to hit anything with that gun, especially since it was my first shot, ever.

"Fine, if that's what you want. But I don't think you want to live with this on your conscience."

"I don't have to, there's not a lot of gas left in the tank."

"Don't talk like that."

"Why? It's the truth, look at me. I'm skinny, pale, I vomit all the time. The nose bleeds and headaches are unbearable. It's almost over. And now it's time to concentrate on us."

There is a lull in the conversation. I know exactly what is going to come out of his mouth next.

"Are you going to tell her?"

"Yes."

 21

Mona is waiting in our suite to tend to my wounds. Her
show of concern supersedes the display of anger she showed at
the bar. Nick dropped me off with a first aid kit he bought on
the way back and then went to his room. I lie on the bed
slowly, nursing my bruises and scrapes. With no adrenaline or
painkillers in my system, I'm starting to realize how banged up
I am. She tugs upward at my shirt and I sit up allowing her to
roll it off over my head. Then she studies my body. It's pale,
gaunt and covered in yellowish purple dents. Deep cuts ooze
blood and puss while scratches show up neon red and pink
against my white skin. She massages my shoulders until I
wince and then she retrieves a bottle of scotch from the dresser.

"You look like you could use a drink."

I take a long swig from the bottle, burning the side of
my tongue where I bit it running.

"I need to know what happened," she says, sitting next
to me and putting her head on my shoulder, careful not to hurt
my tender body.

"I know. No more secrets. But let me say this, if you
want to leave when you know the truth then do so without a

276

fuss. I'm not sure how much longer I have, but I don't have much left in the way of dealing with heartache." I take another swig from the bottle and wait for her reaction. She weaves her fingers through my left hand, clasping tight, and raising it up in front of my face.

"Do you see that ring?"

"Yes."

"Then tell me what happened, husband."

I pause, waiting, why, I'm not sure. This whole trip has become very queer, a warped combination of Dante's *Inferno* and Homer's *Odyssey*, sprinkled with bits of fear and loathing. Hotels disgust me. They all smell the same, empty and alone. For the first time in a long time I miss my apartment, my family, and my job.

"Darin found us and tried to murder me."

Mona springs off of the bed, backing away from me. She backs to the wall beside the teak dresser with a television on it. Staring at the floor she shrinks, sliding down the wall, and grabs her knees while shaking her head. I could only imagine the hell this man was capable of. She never talked about him. The fear in her eyes as I said his name. It was as if the hotel room melted instantly into a savage beating and rape. In the depths of my stomach, like a knife twisting deep inside, I could feel what she feels. Pulling myself off the bed, my legs wobbly, I limp a few feet and fall to the floor. The scotch spills, cauterizing the mud caked cuts on the back of my hand.

On all fours I crawl the rest of the distance and put my arm around her. We stay quiet for a while, save for her sobbing. Then as if struck by lightening she springs to her feet and begins packing.

She targets anything of intrinsic value, post cards, snow globes, jewelry. She shoves things into whatever she can find. Plastic grocery bags. Grease stained McDonalds bags. She shoved some t-shirts into an old pizza box that still had a cold slice in it.

"Come on, we have to leave here!" She shoves a clumped rainbow assortment of panties into a plastic bag from a liquor store.

"Come on, get Nick!" she screams, her voice cracking and getting hoarse. "Come on!"

She grabs her laptop and crams it into a suitcase. She wads up the power cable and stuffs it into a different bag. The inside of her suitcase begins to resemble a homeless person's shopping cart.

"Mona," I stand, take her by the shoulders, and look straight in her eyes. "He's dead. It's done."

Her muscles give out and she folds in half onto the floor in a crying heap. She knew this man for a long time and I don't expect any forgiveness. The abused have a strange way about their abusers. But I need to sleep and give her some space. I collapse into the bed and let the familiar dull firmness of the mattress envelope me.

 22

Over the next few days, Nick and Mona give me some much needed space and time to sleep. Mona shops, scrapbooks, and runs errands. Nick pops in to the hotel room to play video games with me while she is gone. We don't drink as much. I don't drink at all. It's different and in a way it's better. The nightmares about Katrina are gone. In fact, a lot of the guilt I carried over her death feels somehow removed. There is a sense of peace in my spirit. After I killed Darin, so much has changed inside and around me.

Mona doesn't speak of it. But she does have a lightness in her step. A tender touch when changing my bandages. It's like she is suddenly unchained from her past, free to start anew. And Nick is different too. We spend more time with each other, like we used to. Play games in our hotel rooms until the sun comes up. We go for late night walks through the towns we visit, just to talk. It is like we are finally catching up with each other. Sometimes Mona and I lay awake at night and I tell her about my grandparents or my parents. We talk about where we went to high school and our old jobs.

Tonight is just like any other in the past few weeks. Nick and I lay on the bed, pizza slices in one hand, controllers in the other, playing rented games on a console we wired into the hotel's flat screen.

"Hey, since Mona's out, I was wondering if we could talk."

"Sure," he tosses his controller onto the bed and sits upright. "What's up?"

I hesitate, wondering how to proceed. In the past year this guy has done a lot to take care of me, but I haven't really returned the favor. It's time for me to take care of my friends.

"Here." I hand him a folded piece of paper.

"What's this?" he says, unfolding it and squinting at the fine print.

"It's what I'm leaving you, in the event that something happens to me, along with the address to a storage locker that has my things. I want you to have everything."

"Dave, I ..."

"You've driven across the country and been to hell and back with me, it's the least I can do. I realize now that it wasn't the road trip that I needed, it was us. Your companionship. This isn't just my last adventure, this is our last adventure. Together."

"Thanks," he leans in and hugs me. "I'm not even sure what to say ..."

"You don't have to say anything. If anyone has to say anything here, it's me. Thank you Nick. Thank you for coming with me, for having my back. Thanks for everything."

"Dave, come on, it goes without saying."

"I know, but I need you to hear this. And also, I need one more thing," I say, interrupting our moment. "Mona, make sure she's okay. I mean, I have all the faith in the world in her, but she doesn't have anybody. I know sometimes I act like I don't have anybody, but I have an entire family that probably misses me back home. You know that. She actually has no one. Just, please, keep an eye on her."

"Of course."

The next day I wake up early, Mona is already up cutting and pasting pictures in a velvet photo album. I call her over to the bed and she dashes over, tackling me on the mattress. The physical display of affection doesn't even bother my wounds. The sores are numb from my rapidly diminishing supply of painkillers. I sit up in bed and take her by the hands.

"Mona, we need to talk."

"Yeah, I know," she says, as if anticipating my thoughts. "About you and me. And what happened with Darin."

I nod, staying silent, trying to collect my thoughts for the best approach.

"David, before you say anything I want a turn."

"Go on then," I say, squeezing her hands.

"I know how sensitive you are. I see it in your eyes, you carry the weight of the world between those two shoulders. You may try and hide it, but I can see it. And so I know how insane this is going to sound to hear this, but just let it go," she says.

"Murder? Let that go?" I interrupt.

"Murder, but it wasn't murder, was it? It was self-defense." She pauses for a moment, tracing her thoughts. "And, to me, it really doesn't matter what you call it, murder or self defense. Dave, you did this world a favor. I'm free. His wife is free. His children are going to get a fair chance. Anyone who knew him gets a second chance. All because of you."

I'm speechless. It's like she reached in my head and yanked out how I really felt. And that's why she's perfect, in every way. The way she knows what I'm thinking, feeling. It's like we were meant for each other, which we were, because we ended up together. This has all played out exactly how it should. She reaches up and wipes a tear from my eye.

"Thank you," I say, sniffling.

"No, thank you."

23

When we hit the road again, my cancer takes a turn for the worse. I drift in and out of consciousness for a week or two at a time. My migraines are more frequent and last longer. My thoughts are constantly getting lost somewhere between my cerebellum and mouth, sometimes, all I can communicate are slurred vowels.

My appearance isn't much better. My wounds have barely healed, and they won't. When you're this sick, when your immune system is this compromised, you don't heal. There is no getting better. If a bone breaks, you deal with it. A sling, a cast, some pain pills, and no complaining. But, my left eye does open a bit better today than it did the day it was beaten shut.

Sore, I sit upright in bed glancing around the room. Mona is curled up next to me wearing nothing but one of my oversized t-shirts. At this point, it probably looks just as big on me as it does on her. Nick is not in here. I assume he went for either breakfast or dinner, I don't actually know what time it is. The room is immaculate. I told Mona to not worry about cash;

we should at least be comfortable when we aren't on the road. That being said, we've definitely been living here for a while, judging by the small tower of cardboard pizza boxes next to an overflowing trash can full of wrappers, empty cans, and bloody tissues.

One of the empty coffee cups on the floor says Days Inn. This is what the pursuit of the American Dream has brought me. Down and out at a Days Inn, God knows where. I try to stretch but the muscles in my back kink and my spine cracks. My insides don't feel right, like they're resisting my every movement. I slide my feet off the bed and almost knock over a slim chrome trashcan. The bag is missing and it has some puke in it. It's hard to get my balance when I stand up, the spins almost knock me right back down. I grab five or six pills off of the night stand and wash them down with some flat coke. I quickly glance in the mirror and am afraid of what I see. My skin looks like paper and I have lost about 30 pounds.

I limp outside quietly, as to not wake Mona. On my way out I grab a pack of Marlboro Lights from a carton on the dresser. It's morning, I can tell from the smell. The sun is just peeking over the top of the mountainous horizon. Crossing the parking lot to the sidewalk I see that we aren't in a city. The setting is quite awkward, it looks like someone plopped a hotel right in the middle of suburbia, as if they knew I was stopping here on my tour of America.

I smoke a cigarette and once again hope to be a mere shadow on the backdrop of society. My body has begun to really distort my age; I look about 50, so anybody I run into will likely think I am another senior citizen out for a morning walk. I pass a blue ranch style house with a perfectly manicured lawn. Rolls of Kentucky Blue Grass sod, each blade cut to an identical length. A middle-aged man in a red silk bathrobe stands in a sea of asphalt with a newspaper tucked under his arm. Connected to his wrist is a pink leash with a snow white toy poodle on the end of it. The dog is pacing with its back arched, trying to force out shit while the man tells it to go potty.

I can see it, snow globe clear. Everything he will go home to that I will never have. Inside his house is a beautiful wife in a long nightshirt finishing up breakfast. The aroma of home-cooked food will awaken his kids. He takes his eggs over easy and his bacon just a little crispy. She calls up the stairs that breakfast is ready and two kids come charging down to the table. They shovel food into their mouths as he reads his paper and drinks coffee, black of course, like all grown men do. She wraps her arms around him from behind and smiles at what they have built together. Their cookie cutter life where nothing can ever go wrong.

I flick my smoldering cigarette butt onto his lawn. He smiles, in denial, and waves to me from behind his pooping dog. I just stare. They don't even think that across the street

285

there is a young man not getting a fair shot at life. How he only gets enough cash to do something with himself right after he finds out he is going to die. How even when he does get a break the money comes at the cost of the two most important people in his life. How instead of coming to my wedding my parents don't even know I'm married. These upper middle class people make me sick. They don't even have time to break from their perfect little lives to acknowledge a living corpse finishing his cigarette and taking five or six pain killers to stave off death for another day. The final piece of shit falls from his tiny dog's asshole and he produces a Zip-lock bag from his pocket. Wearing the bag like a glove he picks up the warm poop and zips the bag shut.

He's closing his front door when I realize I've been watching him like a zoo exhibit. It's time to get back to my life. To return to my dank tomb of a hotel room. To my accidental wife. To fast food and Oxycontin. I'm walking back when I have an epiphany. This is my perfect life. This is the life I built, with the people I love. It's not any better or worse than his, or anyone else's. It's just different, and that's okay. I lean my hands on the table staring out the window.

"Baby?" Mona says, as she wraps her arms around me from behind. "How was your walk?"

"Fine."

"Are you all right baby?" Her warm body stiffens around me as she lets out a big stretch followed by the most adorable little squeak.

"Yeah, never better."

"Awe, somebody's in a good mood," she says with her head on my shoulder.

"Yeah, well, I've got you. And that's all I need."

She kisses me in the center of my back and then rests her head against the spot she kissed.

"Love you too, baby. Nick was looking for you, he said he's got coffee and bagels in his room."

A few minutes later I can faintly taste the flavors of onion, garlic, and poppy of an "everything" bagel. I'm not sure what this disease is doing to me, but taste is a luxury that's quickly disappearing. I chew my bagel slowly, talking with my mouth full. Nick sips on a large coffee, and stands in the doorway, smoking.

"Where are we?"

"Northern New Mexico," he says.

"Is there anything you want here?"

He shrugs. "Not really, figured we could hole up for a while and buy some time before pressing on to California. You looked like you needed some R-&-R."

"Well, what do you say? Think it's time we see the West Coast and put an end to this odyssey?"

"Absolutely. How's Mona?" Nick leans in close and lowers his voice to a whisper. "We haven't talked since … you know."

"She's good. For the first time in her life she is free."

"Good, then maybe it's time we move. I'll be ready in a few hours."

Later that night, I try to piece together how I ended up in the back seat of the car. The last thing I remember is collapsing in our hotel room. In addition to the headaches, blackouts are becoming almost common place. I've fainted outside a restaurants. Scrapped my knees on asphalt parking lots. Passed out while shopping. The wrought iron squares of a food court table imprinted on my face. The seizures come out of nowhere.

I self-medicate with the last of Spyder's stash. Lorcet, Percadan, Norco, all the pills look the same. A Demoral and Dialaudid cocktail and six hours later I wake up in the car, disoriented. Mystery bruises. The only thing that changes is the scenery. I watch through the passenger window like it is a TV, hidden behind the glass and removed from the world. Status updates from Nick and Mona. We decided to route through Arizona. Some days, I'm only awake long enough to dry heave for an hour. A life lived as a jigsaw puzzle, and the pieces never quite fit together.

"Where are we?" I moan from the backseat. Mona is stroking my hair. Nick looks back from the driver's seat.

"Route 15, somewhere along the Mojave Preserve," he says.

"Let's find a place to rest, I don't feel good."

At the hotel, Nick stands at the counter trying to check in, while Mona does her best to hold me upright. The rag I'm holding under my nose is sopping wet with blood. My right hand is equally soaked and blood is dripping from my fingertips down onto the cement. Even half-conscious I can still see the look of horror on the clerk's face.

"Hey, I was talking to you," Nick snaps his fingers in the clerk's face. "I said we want a room for the night."

"Oh, I'm sorry, is he okay?" The clerk has trouble keeping his eyes off of me.

"He's fine. Listen buddy, are we going to have a problem here?"

"No, I'm sorry, it's just that he looks so …"

Just as the clerk is about to tell me how awful I look my stomach clenches. I push Mona backwards and fall onto my hands and knees spewing chunky vomit all over the grey walkway. The clerk's face turns the color of ash and he looks at his desk to give his eyes a rest. When I'm done Mona and Nick each grab an arm and hoist me back to my feet. Mona smiles big and fake, leaning over the desk, trying to bring the clerk's attention to her cleavage.

"Hello, I'm sorry to be like this but my husband is very sick. He needs to lie down as soon as possible. I know you have your policies, so here."

She reaches into her black purse pulling out my driver's license and two 100 dollar bills. Crisp and folded perfect around my license she slides them across the desk to the clerk.

"Take your time processing the paperwork and keep the change sweetie. I'll be back for his license later."

Without saying anything the clerk hands her a card connected to a plastic keychain.

"Room 42, drive around back."

"Thanks," Nick and Mona say in tandem. I raise my bloody hand and half smile at him. He looks away from me.

Inside the room Mona rifles through Spyder's black drug bag. She pulls out empty pharmaceutical bottles one after another.

"Fuck!" she shouts, throwing an empty bottle of Dilaudid against the wall.

"Ugh … babe calm down," I say, sitting on the bed. "Maybe you two should go out for a bit, pick up some Tylenol PM for me, and some groceries."

She can see it in my eyes. She knows it's time.

"Nick, go outside," she says, wrapping her arms around my neck and pressing her head against my chest. Nick ignores her request, and watches quietly as we embrace. Her tears are soaking through my black t-shirt and dampening my chest.

"Baby, don't cry, it's going to be alright."

"I know," she sniffles.

"Do you need anything while we are out?" Nick asks, giving my shoulder a squeeze. I'm not even mad he stayed here despite her wishes, any true friend would.

"A pack of smokes," I laugh. He smiles and pats me on the back.

"Sure buddy." His eyes are bloodshot, pink around the edges. The tears are too hard to hold back and they travel stubbornly through his stubble along the sides of his face. And then, without another word, he leaves.

"Baby, you've got to get going," I say, doing my best to pry her head from my chest.

"I know, I just want to listen to your heartbeat a little while longer."

What can you say to that? I let her stay with her ear pressed on my chest cavity as long as she needs. After a while she lifts her head and kisses me on the cheek. With what's left of my rapidly depleting strength I place my hands on her cheeks and kiss her for the last time. With my eyes closed I pull away. This is how letting go is. You always want one more. One more cigarette. One more hug. One more kiss. One more precious moment, however short that moment may be.

"I love you," I whisper.

"I love you too," she says, and then she stands and walks out of the room.

Well, this is it. It's down to me and you, tumor. Still sitting up in bed, I fight to stand. The signals my body receives from my brain are heavily distorted and sometimes missing. It's hard to walk, to think. The bathroom door, barely hanging from one hinge, looks a million miles away. I count 12 steps. Twelve awkward and painful steps. I brace myself on everything I can. The bed, the big TV console made of fake wood. I've never seen one of those in a motel room before. Now four terrifying steps with nothing. My vision goes black and I'm left groping along the cracked peeling wallpaper until I find the door frame. I stop, let my vision come back, and go inside, slamming the door shut. I cough deep throaty hacks from the bowels of my lungs, producing gooey phlegm that gums up my mouth like glue.

The coughing fit subsides and I wipe my watery eyes. The turquoise porcelain sink is spattered with chunks of bloody yellow stuff. This last headache feels as though it will split my head in two. A wave of nausea hits, bringing me to my knees almost as fast as it brings my vomit to the floor. When I open my eyes, the puke has more blood in it than undigested food. My cancer is finishing off my internal organs. Chewing them up like a meat grinder as it spreads throughout my body, masticating everything in its path. I fight to sit up in the puddle, and warm wet vomit soaks through my jeans. I push off from the toilet and prop my back against the bathtub. Staring at me from the mirror on the back of the door is the emaciated corpse that was once me.

It's hard to believe it's my reflection. It can't be me. I lift my shirt. My skin is pale, pulled tight against my bones. My sunken eyes have dark bags underneath them. Against my white skin you can trace blue veins. What does Mona think? How could she be attracted to this?

It's hard to breath and the headache is blurring my vision. I'm almost there. I close my eyes and imagine I am sitting in the house I grew up in, at the kitchen table in front of a Scrabble board. The kitchen is empty and drained of color, save for the blending of thick blacks and harsh whites to form a freakish grey. A pulsating, living shade of grey. More alive and more menacing than any storm cloud I've ever seen. I wonder to myself if this is the true face of death, not in a physical form, but in a strange manifestation of color. Scared and alone, I look to my left and out the sliding glass door. Much to my surprise it's not Katrina or Grandma standing outside. It's Mona, with her hands pressed against the glass. The colors outside are vibrant and teaming with a life I have yet to see. A gust of wind, tinged with colors of orange and red, blows Mona's long ebony hair. Thick green fields of grass wave in the wind beyond her. She begins to talk but I can't hear her through the glass. Behind her, standing in the grass

294

are my parents and grandfather, waving to me. Beyond them is Nick. A compulsion starts in my toes, sending shockwaves to my fingertips, beckoning me, pleading me to open the door and step through. I take out a smoke from a pack sitting on the table.

"Not yet."

Did I say that out loud? I open my eyes to a smoking corpse staring at me from the mirror, covered in dried blood and puke. Is this cigarette even real? I muster what little strength I have and pull myself up from the floor and hang myself over the edge of the tub. I can't go to sleep yet, I'm not done. I let cold water run over the back of my head shocking me back to reality. My half-smoked cigarette falls into the tub and swirls in the red water before disintegrating into a swollen filter. I rinse the blood from my hands and pull myself out of the tub, once again staring in the mirror. The sound of the running bath water is soothing.

Is this how the final page in my book will be written? Alone, in a sleazy motel bathroom, somewhere along the road connecting Nevada and California. The smoke stained walls of this fetid place will become my tomb. The wall to my back and cool damp linoleum below my jeans reminds me of the nightmares I used to have. It's fitting that Kat and I should come to end in a similar way. My cancer forced her to take her life in a bathroom, and now, it will take my life in a bathroom. She was strong though, I am not. The mirror on the wall reflects back my own cowardice, I couldn't even kill myself. Always talking such a big game about taking matters into my own hands, about never losing control, but here I am, simply waiting for death's embrace, his cold breath on the back of my neck.

And then everything is clear. This passing thought of Katrina brings with it the key to unlocking the safe buried beneath my subconscious. Things that I have already known but would never admit.

She fucked up. I shout out from my mind to the universe. *She left, on her own terms.*

And that's the truth I would never admit to myself. She left me here, to deal with this all on my own. When I struggled with deciding on how to proceed, she left.

"I was the strong one," I whisper to nobody. It feels good to say it out loud.

Feeling my life slip through the weathered cracks of this filthy floor brings on an even more shocking revelation: I don't want to die today. My stomach pains to even think about it. I don't want to die, but it is okay if I do. I have just one thing left I must do. With labored movements I slide out a tattered and stained envelope from my back pocket. It's time to make peace. I pull out the folded letter. I hold the yellow, ruled paper in front of me, stare at it's cursive handwriting. I pick up my lighter from the floor and flick on its tiny flame. I watch it dance for a minute and then touch it to the corner of

296

the letter. It's time I let go of this burden. The letter is engulfed in flames, burning my fingertips as I drop it in the bathtub. The smoke sets off the fire alarm and I hear raised voices outside the bathroom door.

The door bursts open.

Standing in the doorway is Nick and Mona. EMT's push past them and start hooking things up to me. I blink and look around. No blood, no vomit. An illusion brought on by something, maybe cancer, maybe withdrawals. There is nothing in here but me and a smoldering letter and cigarette butt in the bathtub. Mona kneels next to me.

"I broke my promise," I say through an oxygen mask.

"It's okay, baby." She smiles through teary eyes.

They wheel me out of the hotel room on a gurney while Mona walks along, still holding my hand.

"Where are they taking me?" I ask her.

"We're going to the hospital, and then we're going to get you home."

"Home."

That word finally puts a smile on my face.

25

It took her four years to arrive at this doorstep. She had the address but not the nerve. Plus, he had told her he didn't know what she'd find. At worst, nobody. Or people with different names, wondering who this crazy lady is. At best he said she might find what she was looking for, a family. He sent her to find them because she deserved it. They deserved it. She stood in front of the red painted door, not sure what she was waiting for. The strap of a black duffel bag wrapped around her right hand. Her left squeezing the hand of their child.

Beyond this door was part of a life she had always imagined. A middle-aged woman dicing celery on an old cutting board. Scraping it into a mixing bowl with tuna and mayonnaise. A man sitting in his den, carefully assembling a delicate ship in a tiny glass bottle. On the living room couch sits an elderly man, the television at full volume to compensate for his hearing loss. He watches TV instead of working on cars, his tired, arthritic hands no longer able to turn a wrench.

Inside the house is a family who would welcome her and the child. They would fill the hole in their hearts.

She stretches out her hand, extends her index finger, depresses the doorbell. She feels it ring throughout her body like an electric shock of anxiety and relief. Before she can completely process what she has just done, the door opens.

In front of her is the woman, paring knife in hand, staring quizzically. Studying the two of them. The girl's hopeful smile. The child and his striking familiarity. This nagging sense that they know each other. A sense that this young girl and her child are here to open a new chapter in the stalled-out story of their lives.

"Can I help you dear?" she asks, stepping outside the door.

"Hi." Her brain stutters, out of fear of the brave new world staring her in the eyes.

The little boy tugs at her sleeve.

"Is this Grama?" he innocently blurts out, wide-eyed and smiling.

The woman takes a step back, as if the words of the child were carried by a gale force wind. The girl is equally caught off guard by her son's ice breaker.

"I know you," the woman says, sensing the girl's unease. "You work at the VA my father-in-law goes to, you're a nurse right?"

"Well, not exactly. I work there part-time while I'm going to school to get my nursing license back. I moved here three years ago, I have an apartment downtown."

That the woman ignored the little boy's outburst calms her anxiety.

"Do you want to tell me what brings you here?"

No, she didn't. She wanted to scream and run away. She wanted to un-ring that doorbell, take her child, and run from the unknown. She wanted her husband here, by her side, to tell their story together. But she didn't have any of that. All she has is the child, and he deserves a family. Now she knows just how he felt, keeping secrets for so long.

Deep breath.

"My name is Mona, and this is your grandson, David."

The woman knew this all along, but hearing it overflowed her heart with joy. Tears fill the woman's eyes and she drops the paring knife to the ground, pulling the girl into a hug.

"Nick said you were out there. He said you were afraid, and that he'd lost touch with you." Her words are borderline gibberish, coming fast and mixed with sobs. "You were right under our noses the whole time!"

She was squeezing Mona so tight she forgot about the small child. She lets go of Mona and kneels to get a good look at the boy.

"But Nick didn't say anything about you, little man." She grabs David and hugs him tight.

"Nick doesn't know," Mona says.

"Hush, it doesn't matter. The only thing that matters is that you're here now, you're home. Grab your things and come in. I'm sure you have a long story to tell."

A long story indeed.